STEVEN DECKER

ADDICTED TO TIME

Book 3 of the *TIME CHAIN* series

STEVEN DECKER

Copyright © 2023 by Steven Decker

All rights reserved.

No part of this publication may be reproduced, distributed, or transmitted in any form or by any means, including photocopying, recording, or other electronic or mechanical methods, without the prior written permission of the publisher, except as permitted by U.S. copyright law. For permission requests, visit www.stevendecker.com.

The story, all names, characters, and incidents portrayed in this production are fictitious. No identification with actual persons (living or deceased), places, buildings, and products is intended or should be inferred.

Quotes of scripture are from the World English Bible.

ISBN 979-8-9873940-7-6 (print)
ISBN 979-8-9873940-4-5 (eBook)

Library of Congress Control Number: 2023909013

Book Cover by Sabrina Milazzo
Interior design and formatting by Sabrina Milazzo

First edition 2023

Visit the author's website at www.stevendecker.com
Published by TIER Books LLC

Novels by Steven Decker

Distant Finish

The Time Chain Series:
　Time Chain
　The Balance of Time
　Addicted to Time

The Another Kind Series:
　Child of Another Kind
　Earth of Another Kind
　Gods of Another Kind
　Genesis of Another Kind

Walking Into Dreams

For the good in all of us.

Chapter 1

The Planet of Terrene | Earth Year 2257

I realize that after some of the things I've done, many of you must despise me, but no matter your feelings toward me, you must admit that I have also done some good. And if I may be so bold, I would say that more good than bad has resulted from my existence. We cannot ignore the fact that good prevailed, admittedly, because I was brought to heel before ending the world. Still, you must know that I was not myself at the time, far from it, so to cast dispersions on my character while I was under the influence of potent medicine, well, I urge you to read on. Herein you will gain a much greater understanding of the situation and hopefully foster some semblance of empathy for me. And I assure you, I am perfectly sane now. Stable as a workhorse in old Ireland, my friends, with only one goal in life. To do good. Always good.

Please allow me to tell you some things you don't know about me, some of which might surprise you. I promise to do it quickly because events have transpired on Terrene, on Earth, and beyond, which I must urgently report to you. There is some good news, and yes, some bad as well, I'm afraid to say. But first, the short version of my life.

I was born in the countryside of England in the year 2149. This was when England was still England, well before the founding of EarthGov in 2173. Ironically, the year 2149 was the year OIM was invented. Ironic because, as you well know, I am not only the foremost expert in the growth and AI infusion of Organic Intelligent Material but the only biological human in the universe who can speak directly to OIM. Yes, OIM's inventors, the uploaded minds, can talk to it as well, but they don't seem as adept at bending it to their will as I am. That may be because the Community of Minds is kept in check by the biological humans who maintain the facility in which they are housed, the tremendous black monolith which rests in the now unused time station in the Time Management building, or it may be simply that the OIM knows it's true master. I am a brother of OIM, part OIM in fact, due to my dangerous yet successful experiments to make myself immortal, which I'm happy to report, I am.

But I digress. You must understand the why of all this, so you must first learn more about me. My birthplace was the small town of Ambleside in the north-west of England. Ambleside sits at the northern shores of Lake Windermere, England's largest lake, and is within the borders of England's largest national park, the Lake District. It is an ancient place and still looked that way when I was growing up there. OIM would not encroach on my historic village for many years after it had covered most of the world because Ambleside had roots. The Romans had taken an interest in it all the way back in the first century, and the remains of their Galava Fort were still present. The Bridge House, a tiny home made of stone that sat on a bridge that spanned a brook, also stood firm during my childhood. Built in the 17th century by the Braithwaite family, it served so many roles over the centuries it was hard to remember them all—a counting house for the mills, a tea room, a weaver's shop, a cobblers, and even a home for a family of eight at one point. Most of the buildings in the town center were still made of stone back in the 2150s, with weathered slate roofs. The road that ran through town had become a pedestrian mall, and tourists milled about, unworried about any vehicle that might hit them, because automobiles were gone by then, supplanted by hovercraft that flew above all the buildings and came down for landings in spaces that were similar to parking lots of old.

    The number of full-time residents in Ambleside was around three thousand when I lived there, although there were always many thousands more than that in town, taking into account the tourists and the students from the local university. And while the village was peppered with pubs and restaurants, the terrain surrounding it was rugged country. A climb up Scafell Pike on a clear day provided views all the way Scotland in the north, Wales in the south, and across the Irish Sea to the Emerald Isle in the west. The wilderness stretched out in every direction, and nearly 2,500 square kilometers of it had been preserved in perpetuity, as the Lake District National Park, centuries ago.

    I was free to roam the hills, which, although vast and unforgiving, contained very little wildlife that could actually hurt a little boy, and I had a tracker embedded in my arm, which enabled my parents to know where I was if they cared to check. For me, the best feature of the tracker was its reverse function, which allowed me to send an alarm to them if I found myself in an untenable situation. I'm not sure my parents felt the same way about this, however, as I ended up using that alarm more than they would have liked.

    But there was one adventure I took where I didn't have to call my parents to be rescued, even though so many aspects of that day of mischief could have led to a call for help. It was the day I decided to scale Scafell Pike by myself when I was nine. I'll never forget that day, and it had nothing to do with the sense of accomplishment one would typically attribute to a successful solo climb of the Pike at the age of nine. No, it was something else entirely.

Chapter 2

It was a weekday, so I waited patiently while my parents got ready for work, finally leaving my brother and me alone in the house, presumably to study. My brother was fourteen at the time and was charged with keeping an eye on me, so I knew I'd have to slip away unnoticed when I was ready. First, I prepared the things I would need: a large bottle of water, some energy bars, a ham and cheese sandwich, some crisps, a fresh apple, and a small first aid kit, just in case. I placed all of my provisions into a daypack and put on clothes appropriate for the wilderness, including flexible walking trousers, a t-shirt, and a long-sleeve shirt on top of that, plus an all-weather jacket. It was late spring, so it could still be quite chilly at the summit of Scafell Pike. Once ready, I slunk quietly out of the house, tip-toed down the porch stairs, and hurried along the walkway and out into the street. I heard no noise from inside, so I assumed my brother was hard at work on his studies, oblivious to my status, which was the usual way of things when my brother was studying. Unlike me, he was a highly dedicated student, and when he was in his lessons, his concentration was so profound that he was unaware of anything else happening around him.

The next phase of my adventure, finding a way to get to Scafell Pike, nearly twenty-five kilometers away, involved going to town and seeing who I might cajole into helping me. I was well-known to all the shopkeepers in the village, as I always seemed to want something in their stores for which I didn't want to pay, and I knew any one of them would immediately turn me in to my parents if I asked them for help on this particular, somewhat questionable activity. I was therefore forced to visit the street corner where some of the least distinguished youth of our town often congregated. These were the children of parents who had been wards of the state their entire lives, as had been their parents and grandparents before them. It was almost expected that each generation would follow suit, dropping out of school at age sixteen, failing to secure employment of any kind, and gathering, as a rite of passage into official lethargy, on the street corner outside of the convenience store, the same place their own parents had gathered during their teenage years as well.

There were seven of them milling about there. Five boys and two girls. I want to say they were aged sixteen to nineteen, but I didn't know; after all, I was only nine. I did see that they were all heavily tattooed and scantily clad, and what little clothing they did have was exceptionally tight. Tight was already in vogue in the 2150s, and it only became more so whenced the Minds invented the clothing pills later that century. Several of the mob in front of me were smoking some cigarettes; whatever the latest trend was, the only thing sure was that it wasn't tobacco, long since an extinct crop by virtue of laws and regulations and the diversity of synthetic alternatives, which were readily available. For all I knew, those kids were smoking synthetic opium. It was all out there, but as I said, I was nine. Didn't know and didn't care.

I was probably more intelligent than all seven of these lunks combined, and even though my crypto account was small, it probably held more units than all of these freeloaders together had, if they even had crypto accounts. Bottom line: I had what they didn't have, and they knew it. They weren't going to beat me up to get it, however, because violent crime was virtually non-existent in 2158 in jolly old England, wiped out by a social safety net that took care of everyone, even deadbeats like these lot. What they had that I wanted was a hoverboard, and it was sitting against the white stucco wall of the convenience store right behind them.

The largest of them stepped up to me. "Skippin' our lessons, are we now pee-wee?" he asked, getting some chuckles from his friends.

"Why yes, I most certainly am," I replied. "I didn't catch your name, sir."

"Didn't give it." He had his arms on his waist now, one knee crooked out to the side like he was losing his patience with me already.

"So you didn't," I replied. "My name is Charles Burke, and I'd like to pay you a handsome sum of money to borrow your hoverboard."

"Oh, do you now, fancy boy?" he asked. More chuckles from the crowd.

"Yes, I do," I said, undeterred. "I'm taking a day trip to Scafell Pike and would like to rent the board for around eight hours. You have my word that I will return it here promptly at six o'clock this evening. How much would you charge for such a short-term lease, sir?"

"Not my board," he said. "'At's Harry's board." He pronounced the boy's name as Arry. "What say ye, Harry? Interested?" The head man raised his eyebrows when looking at poor Harry, a slight boy with his hair greased up into a pyramid on top of his tiny head, nodding to Harry that he would indeed be interested in renting out his board.

"That'll be a hundred quid, mate," said Harry, winking at the big boss.

"I'm afraid that's a bit steep, sir," I replied. To give you a feel for how steep that was, one hundred pounds in 2158 was enough to buy a used hoverboard like Harry's, although that wasn't an option for me. You had to be sixteen to own one of the things. "I was thinking ten would cover it."

The entire crowd of losers laughed heartily. But I was not at all disheartened. I had read how to negotiate in an online blog, so I smiled, thanked them, and turned around to leave.

"Hold on now, you little ragamuffin!" came the leader's voice. "We'll take fifty, and you can keep the board until tomorrow, same time."

"Thank you, sir. I appreciate your consideration. But my budget for this rental is twenty-five pounds. I'm afraid it's all I have." This, of course, was a lie, but it was true that twenty-five pounds was my self-imposed limit, based on my own calculation that I'd be willing to pay twenty-five percent of the price of a used board for the rental. I looked over at the hoverboard, nicked and scarred, obviously an old model. There was no doubt that it was used. Terribly used.

The leader scrunched his lips, making an expression indicating he was unhappy with my offer, but then he relented. "Give him the board, Harry," he said.

Harry handed me the board, and I took it and set it down. The leader held out his handy, and I pressed mine on top of his, dispensing the money. He checked to see if the amount was correct, then nodded. I immediately stood on the board, and it lifted into the air. As I flew away from them, I called out. "See you same time tomorrow then, mates!"

It took me about an hour to get to the trailhead for Scafell Pike. I only dared travel up to twenty-five kilometers per hour as I'd only ridden a hoverboard once or twice in the past and never for such a distance. I kept the board half a meter off the ground and used a combination of two-lane roads and walking trails to reduce the distance to Wasdale Head, the trailhead at the bottom of the mountain I planned to use to begin the ascent. When I arrived at Wasdale, I got off the board, and it settled down onto the ground. I picked it up, looked around to see if anyone was about, and once satisfied, I went up the trail a few yards, stepped off the track, and hid the board under a broad bush. Now I could walk.

I took the Brown Tongue Path up. This was well-known to be the most direct route, and I was pressed for time as it was nearly noon. If I was quick about it, I could make it to the top in around three hours. I followed the trail, which Lake District workers had kindly enhanced by placing flat stones on much of the lower route, but as I got higher, these smooth pavers gave way to rocky trails, interspersed with tufts of grass, growing taller now that spring had nearly birthed summer. If I am honest, I tell you that the path up was a bit boring, and I began to wonder if the most exciting part of my journey would end up being the negotiation with the thugs down on the street corner in Ambleside, or perhaps when I returned the hoverboard to them the following morning. But then I arrived at the final ascent to the top of the Pike, and things got a bit more dicey. It was steep, rocky terrain, and I found myself on all fours from time to time, negotiating my way up through the boulder field.

I was winded when I finally reached the summit and surprised that I was alone up there. However, it wasn't the summer holiday season; it was a weekday, so that explained it. The day was clear, and while the wind slapped my face fairly briskly, it wasn't a hurricane and was easily tolerable. At the same time, I enjoyed the view of Wales to the south, Scotland to the north, and Northern Ireland across the Irish Sea, all in sight from the top of Scafell Pike on that late-spring day. The view assuaged my boredom somewhat, although I wasn't looking forward to the descent. It was past three o'clock, and I needed to head back soon, or I'd be in trouble at home for missing dinner. Not that I wouldn't be in trouble at home soon, anyway. I was sure my brother had discovered my absence by now, and it really was a role of the dice as to whether or not he'd alerted my parents, but the lack of a call to my handy indicated he was waiting it out. If I hurried, I might escape my parents' wrath this time.

I sat down on a boulder to eat my sandwich. I needed some fuel in the engine to make it back down, and as I sat there, a miraculous thing happened. A man appeared from nowhere and seemed as if he were no ordinary man. He was tall but muscular, his physique easy to see since his yellow clothing was as tight to his skin as the tattoos were to the wayward youth down in Ambleside. His straight hair was dark and long, pinned back in a ponytail that dropped well down his back. He seemed a bit out of it for a few seconds, but then he gathered his bearings and began to enjoy the view, not having laid eyes on me as of yet. He slowly turned in a circle, and eventually, he saw me, and a smile crept onto his face as if he might know me. And then he disappeared.

I finished my sandwich and left the top of the Pike in a hurry, wondering the whole way down what I'd just witnessed. Was the man a ghost, a figment of my imagination, or something else? I didn't know, but it was a memory I'd carry with me my entire life, and eventually,

STEVEN DECKER

I figured out that the man I saw on top of Scafell Pike that day was me.

Chapter 3

Ambleside was a wonderful place for an adventurous child like myself to grow up, cut short, unfortunately, by the untimely deaths of my parents. Mum and Dad were professors at the university in town. They kept me out of the local public schools, opting instead to teach me using AI tutors, which were readily available and superior in most ways to traditional teaching methods, as long as the student was willing to participate. For my part, I loved learning from an early age, and while I was prone to mischief if left to my own devices, my older brother, William, was always there to make sure I followed the lesson plans, well most of the time, anyway (snicker, snicker). William was five years older than me, and I adored him, as would any younger brother. I was around ten when it became clear that I was much brighter, academically speaking, than William since, at that point, we were doing the same lesson plan. William wasn't behind—he'd end up at a fine university when he was only seventeen—but I was far ahead of other children my age.

When I was twelve, both my parents died, killed by one of the many plagues that would sweep the Earth every decade or so until the immunity pills were invented a few years later by the uploaded minds. I loved my parents and suffered, as would any twelve-year-old, from their loss, and as I look back on that trauma, from my viewpoint now, as a 108-year-old man, I realize that horrible event was the first building block of my addiction to time. Here were two vibrant people, both in their mid-forties, wiped from existence by the vagaries of the cruel world in which we all lived. I think something registered in my subconscious then, that I would not let the same fate befall me. On the contrary, I would laugh in the face of death, daring it to try and take me. And now, of course, it never will.

After my parents died, I was shipped off to a boarding school for advanced children and spent four years there before I enrolled at Cambridge at the age of sixteen on a full academic scholarship. Like my father, I pursued biology; like my mother, I pursued chemistry. Yes, I obtained degrees in both disciplines in three years, and at the age of nineteen, I enrolled in graduate studies of what would become my life's passion—OIM. I wrote and defended my dissertation—AI Infusion Reimagined—at the age of twenty-two, walking away not only with a PhD in OIM Science but as a world-renowned authority on state-of-the-art methods of infusing AI into OIM. My dissertation became the foundation of the new methodology for AI infusion, replacing the old, hit-or-miss process of infusing AI into OIM samples that had already been grown with a method of attaching AI instructions at the cellular level, essentially allowing the AI and the OIM to be fused at the moment of the OIM's birth as a living entity.

The year I obtained my PhD was 2171, two years before the founding of EarthGov. I was immediately employed, at a ridiculously high salary and with stock options in hand, by a firm that wanted to commercialize OIM for making things—OIMtech, it was called. Within two years, the firm went public on the London Stock Exchange, and I became rich. We were successful at building virtually anything we set out to make. An AI team within the firm would write the code for what we wanted to create, then give it to my team, of which I was the head, and we would convert the AI into a chemical code the OIM cells could receive and understand, using the methods I had developed for my dissertation. The OIM could then be grown into anything we could write code for, virtually everything.

When the EarthGov complex in Brussels was planned, our firm was contracted to build it. The process amazed the people at the highest levels of the world government, and they became particularly enamored with me, as I was now the CEO. I discovered that I was not only good at the technical aspects of OIM growth and AI infusion but also had a knack for sales. Something about my personality and the tone of my voice, along with my British accent, made people like me. So even when I was elevated by the board of directors to CEO, I made a point of being the primary salesperson for all the big jobs. Since EarthGov was now our largest client, I became well-known to all the high-ranking government officials.

I'd also like to speak a bit more about people liking me. Those of you who know me are well aware that I am a thief and a murderer, and I have killed people who got in my way and been captured and imprisoned. Yet, I have not only regained my freedom, but I have also maintained friendships with many who've witnessed my worst atrocities, up close and personal, and even some of my intended victims who managed to survive, such as Dani and Aideen, still have an affection for me. I'll speak about those two soon, but before that, I'd like to tell you about the love of my life. Annette Li.

Time travel was invented by the Community of Minds in 2183. I was a thirty-four-year-old billionaire and had fallen in love with one of my assistants a few years prior. Annette was brilliant, ambitious, and beautiful. We'd both taken the pills by the time we met, so we looked thirty, but Annette's actual age at the time was thirty-six, so she was a few years older than me. I was utterly taken with her in every way.

Our romance had not happened immediately. Annette had been working for my company for years when we finally came together. I'd noticed her from the start. At first, it was mere physical attraction. She was a beautiful woman. An American of Asian descent, she was on the taller side, with a trim, shapely body and that long, shimmering dark hair. I hadn't known her before she took the pills, so I don't know if her skin had been so smooth and glowingly perfect before, but it certainly was when I first saw her, and it radiated waves of sensuality. At least for me it did. Another thing that was particularly captivating about Annette was her voice. Soft, melodic, almost hypnotic, calming when I was agitated, and arousing when we were alone together, behind closed doors.

It turned out, however, that physical attraction ended up paling in comparison to my interest in Annette's intelligence. She majored in chemistry and political science as a Stanford undergrad and then went on to post-graduate work at my alma mater, Cambridge, where she obtained her PhD in the same field I had done, OIM Science. She rose up through the ranks of OIMtech rapidly and without any special favors from me and ultimately ended up attending many meetings where I was present. At that point, I could wait no longer. I offered her a job as my Executive Vice President, a role that had recently become open. She would be my right-hand person going forward and deserved the position, regardless of my personal feelings. The last thing I wanted was for her to feel she hadn't earned the promotion; frankly, just being in her presence was enough for me for a long time. But I came to believe that my feelings might be reciprocated. Those beautiful brown eyes just bored into my own as if they were searching for what lay behind them, trying to get to know the real me. Eventually, I convinced myself I needed to find out, and if I was deluding myself, I would leave my infatuation out of our relationship.

We dined together regularly as part of our professional responsibilities, sometimes with dignitaries of Earth-Gov and other times just the two of us. Still, I wanted her to know how I felt, so one evening, when we were at dinner alone, I asked her out on a date. I clarified that if it made her uncomfortable, I would never bring up the topic again, and I meant it. Her response astounded and confused me.

"Aren't we kind of on a date right now, Charles?" she asked.

I stumbled with my answer, thrown off by her initial response. "Well, um, not really," I said. "I mean, I want you to know that I try to keep the professional, um, separate from the personal." And then she threw me further off my game.

"If I were to suggest that you come to my room when we finish dinner, you'd have to turn me down since this isn't an official date?"

"Why, um, no, I suppose you're right," I said, regaining my footing somewhat.

"So?"

"Well, yes, certainly. A jolly good idea!"

For a few years, Annette and I shared the most fulfilling time of my life from both a professional and a personal perspective. But when time travel was invented in 2183, we were offered the contract to build the first time station, and things began to change. I had found a new love—time travel—but I wanted it not only for myself but for Annette as well. And that is where she drew the line. She refused to join my effort to "acquire" the technology and turned me into the EarthGov authorities. I was left with no choice but to abscond with the tech and disappear, and in one instant, I went from billionaire tech mogul in love to on-the-run fugitive, never quite able to regain my former status. It is also true that I killed a few people who tried to stop me, accidentally, as I will explain in a moment, and while I regret that unfortunate outcome to this day, I learned then just how far I was willing to go, not only to maintain my freedom but to keep on living.

You also know what happened to Annette while I was relegated to obscurity and running for my life. She ingratiated herself with the EarthGov authorities, and it wasn't long before she was one of the most influential people on Earth. I must admit, I was hurt. Terribly injured, actually. Now I'm not blaming anything on her—I take full responsibility for my own actions—but it was Annette's betrayal that began my slow spin downward to insanity.

Chapter 4

When I was approached by EarthGov about building the first time station, my first thought was that I could use time travel to go back to 2161, to when I was twelve. I could give my parents the immunity pills, so they wouldn't die from the plague. I didn't consider the effect that might have on my future, or on the future in general, but since I ended up as one of the most influential people of all time, I suppose it would have had a significant impact if my parents had actually taken the pills and lived, although what effect that might have engendered, I had no idea. But speculation on that result turned out to be moot because when I took my first time mission after I had stolen the technology, appearing to my parents as a thirty-year-old Charles from the future, they refused me. They actually told me to get out of their house and never come back. It was my greatest failure as a salesman; I couldn't even convince them I was their son.

Some firmly believe that I built the Time Chain to find a thread in the past which I could change, to create leverage for myself in the present, and ultimately become the most powerful person in the world. It ended up at that, but that's not how it started. It started with me searching for my ancestors. My father's family tree stretched back into Ireland, and my mother's into Denmark, so I spent a lot of time in both places. Locating the station beneath the channel between Omey Island and Claddaghduff had nothing to do with my heritage on my father's side; it was simply a great hiding place, one that I had visited with my parents as a child and remembered as being deliciously isolated. And it was convenient as I went further back in time when no air travel existed because it gave me easier access to my father's side of the family, but that wasn't the rationale behind its location. It was just a damn hard place to find.

As I consider why it was vital for me to use time travel to learn about people from my family that I would not have otherwise known, I think it centered on my need for acceptance. My parents were always good to me—although they adhered to the English tradition of keeping things more formal than necessary, even in familial relationships—and I can't make the case that I faced rejection as a child, leading to insecurities as an adult manifesting in a need for acceptance. There's no doubt I wanted more affection from my parents, but I didn't feel rejected by them until I went back to try and save them. That repudiation was profound, and while comprehensible for a rational person, my rationality was already leaving me even in the early days of time travel. I think I went to find my parents' ancestors to try and learn the why of it. Why couldn't they recognize their own son when he came to save them? What was it about these people that made them so suspicious of strangers? Crazy, I admit. And my obsession didn't last. I met my great grandparents, and my great, great grandparents, etc., never telling them who I really was, and found them to be, well, boring. They were just people. Nothing would be gleaned or gained by getting to know them.

All the while, I was being pursued by EarthGov authorities for stealing their most precious technology. Hence my attention soon turned to self-preservation and the ultimate rationale of defeating my enemy by conquering them. The heart of this new objective, of course, was the rejection by Annette. I should clarify, however, what happened back then, and when, because you need to know the truth. First, I took a sample of the time travel OIM, immediately telling Annette, who I trusted completely, explaining to her that I wanted to use it to save my parents from the plague. She seemed sympathetic to my cause, but the next thing that happened was a team of military personnel showing up at the OIMtech offices, seeking to arrest me. I had a variety of security systems installed at OIMtech, for apparent reasons: after all, I was the inventor of the technology being used to infuse OIM with AI, and I needed to protect it.

The security systems ranged from simple alarms to offensive systems that would disarm and incapacitate an intruder. Suddenly, four soldiers stormed into my office, weapons raised and telling me to stand and put my hands up. I had no choice but to comply, but as I slowly stood, I discretely flicked a switch on the underside of my desk. There were three switches: one for stun, one for severe stun, and one for kill. Frankly, I'd never used them before—there had been no need to—and had no idea which switch was which. My fingers flipped the one that killed, and that is what happened. I wanted to stun them, but I ended up killing them. To this day, I view that incident as one of my greatest sins against humanity, and I still intend to rectify that situation if and when the opportunity presents itself.

So clear away all your preconceived notions about my intentions at that time. I simply wanted to save my parents, and no one was going to stop me from trying. Would you let someone stop you if the opportunity to keep your parents from a horrible death presented itself to you? Annette obviously turned me in, and it has never been clearly stated, until now, that I wasn't trying to destroy the world, I wasn't trying to end mind uploading, I wasn't trying to become the world's only expert in the growth and infusion of OIM and in time travel and I wasn't trying to become immortal, at that time. All of that came much later after I fled and began living the life of a fugitive, after my parents rejected me, claiming I was an imposter when my only intention was to save them. All those horrible things I did came later, as I watched from afar while the love of my life rose in power, ultimately attaining her current position, all at my expense and simply because I had trusted her. Everything I did after that was to exact revenge on her, and admittedly, things got out of hand, especially when I began ingesting OIM.

As I mentioned, the OIM experiments I performed happened much later. Yes, I informed Annette, the Minister of Time Management by then, because I was making so much progress in the mammalian trials and was confident the government would want me to begin working for them again. I explained that the soldiers had been killed in self-defense, but Annette would hear nothing of it and denied my every offer to help the world become a better place. Her response was always the same: turn myself in, and then we could talk about it. It hurt so much that I began using time travel to find a way to destroy Annette, going back in the past and searching for ways to wipe her from existence without wiping myself and others out as well. I must admit, I had no idea what I was doing. Even my powerful mind could never predict the direction and size of the time ripples from events I had contemplated. And it was slow going. Trips to the past took time and planning, and the years began to pass more quickly. I decided that I could no longer wait to become immortal, so I began ingesting the OIM, with good results, except I could not see that I was progressively becoming more unstable and, ultimately, completely unhinged.

I convinced myself I was fully justified in destroying the world by destroying the Mind Upload Community before it got started, and when that seemed impossible, I conceived the idea of infecting the world's OIM and going to this Utopia Annette was building in 2585. And I got very close to pulling it off, but Dani conspired with Annette and ruined my plan. Thank goodness they did. As I've mentioned, I was not myself at that time. But as you know, I escaped and traveled back to 1801, still verifiably insane and armed with the time travel tech and the time link I needed (Orla) to try again. But once again, Dani, and one of my oldest friends, Aideen, conspired against me, and again, I am so thankful they did. Because I wouldn't be here today, on my beloved Terrene, the planet I brought back to life for the Land People and for the people of Earth. Dani and Aideen are here, and together we have faced many adversaries, perhaps none so powerful as the one I will tell you about next, my beloved Annette.

Chapter 5

Annette visited Terrene in early 2257, not long after Aideen's clone went to live on Earth, and she brought a military contingent the size of a platoon. At least twenty-five soldiers on a supposedly friendly, purely observational, diplomatic mission. And it's not like she needed them. There were at least fifty soldiers here from the original mission, and all of them were loyal to Earth. To her. But I suppose she wasn't sure about that, and when I read her thoughts and learned of her intention to destroy my time station, I realized why. It was true that the soldiers of Terrene Base One had become fond of the place, and its people, including me (especially me! I was a hero, after all), but in the end, they were loyal to their command structure, which originated on Earth. They would not take up arms against Annette; therefore, she could go to my house any time she chose to and destroy my work. As it turned out, she took her time.

The soldiers left her side and went to the barracks outside of town, where most of the original military lived. Annette tried to pretend she was just one of the gang, visiting Murphy's pub and hanging out with her old friends, Dani and Aideen, and of course, Orla and Liam. I was also invited, and I played along, not showing the cards I was already holding. Annette retired early, allegedly tired from her long journey (which took a few seconds, at least!), but the rest of us stayed on at Murphy's, as we always did. It was a rare night when any of us left before 15 a.m., midnight, and this night was no exception. Murphy's was the social epicenter of our world, as Liam had predicted from the beginning. That a man from the 18th century, who hadn't spent a sober waking moment for the entirety of his adult life, could envision how important his pub would be to literally all of the residents of Base One on Terrene, humans and Land People alike, really says something about the man that goes beyond understanding. To this day, I am baffled by his accuracy.

But Liam worked hard to make the pub a success. There was no smell of stale beer or burnt food in Murphy's. The place smelled clean because it was. Liam and Orla saw to that. They put in the hours, eighteen a day, on average. They had to because the pub was open, officially, for seventeen of Terrene's thirty-hour days.

It opened at 15 p.m., which was noon, and closed at 2 a.m., seventeen hours later. I realize this seems excessive, but the bodies all of us from Earth had, having taken the immunity pills and the youth pills, gave us the energy to work as long as we wanted, and for Liam and Orla, it wasn't work. It was life! And if they went to bed at 4 a.m. and slept until 14 a.m., they could have a full ten hours of sleep anyway, which was more than any of us slept. We simply didn't need it.

Long waking hours were even more the case for the Land People. Their race had been natives of the planet until they were exiled some six hundred or more years previously by the Water People, but when they went to space on their diaspora, they kept the thirty-hour clock. Why wouldn't they? The Land People were also famous drinkers. Their bodies processed alcohol differently than human bodies, and they hardly felt it when they slugged down a pint of ale. Most Land People could drink a dozen or more ales and show no ill effect. Those who wanted to get drunk drank the Irish Whiskey, which would do the job for them, although it took quite a few of those for them to actually get tipsy.

But I was telling you about Annette coming to Terrene to destroy my time station. And yes, I was hot about it and needed to express my feelings to someone. As always, Dani and Aideen were there for me.

They always were, God bless them. But Aideen was tied up in some kind of heated conversation with Clarion, so I pulled Dani aside and spoke softly, even though the Land People who were present could read my thoughts, which was one of the biggest reasons why there were no secrets on Terrene. People didn't realize it, but the Land People were bigger gossips than humans! Anyway, back to my conversation with Dani.

"Do either of you know why Annette's here?" I asked, and I must have uttered those words with a tone of vehemence in my voice because Dani looked somewhat taken aback.

"Why the intensity Charles?" asked Dani. "And no, we don't know any more than you do. Less, it seems. What have you heard?"

"I have heard only the thoughts in Annette's mind," I said. "And her primary mission seems to be destroying my time station!"

Dani seemed to be pondering my revelation. I wasn't reading her mind, but I'm sure she wondered just how far this ability had developed within me. And for the record, it wasn't a very advanced form of mind reading; I could only pick up thoughts screaming loudly in another person's mind. And I wasn't anxious to employ it as a means of gaining some kind of advantage over others. But in the case of Annette's "Diplomatic Mission" to Terrene, I had my own self-interest in mind, and sure enough, she was there to inflict further harm on me, as if what she'd already done wasn't enough. And Dani, being the true friend she'd become, tried to help me work through the issue.

"Charles, do you have any plans for using the time station any further? I mean, is there a reason you want to keep it?"

"Absolutely," I said. "I'm finally in a position to use time travel for good purposes, which is what I intend to do, and here comes Annette, ready to snatch it away from me."

"What, specifically, did you have in mind?" she asked, a skeptical tone in her voice.

"One thing I know for certain is that I want to go back in time and save all the people I killed."

"That's quite noble, Charles, but it sounds complicated. Because of the old tech you use, you need a time link to get you to all those times and places. A time link who was there at the same time you were."

"Yes, I know," I said, but I didn't reveal that I already knew how to get around that glitch.

"How many people was it, Charles?" asked Dani.

"Well, there were the four soldiers in my office. And the two time travelers from Sadiki's station who tried to capture me in 1801. And I've had dreams about a man I killed in Liam's cottage, someone helping you and Aideen to rescue Orla."

"That was James, her husband," said Dani. "I've had those dreams too. Annette explained that it happened in another reality that was changed by capturing you before you had the chance to kill James. You were also going to kill me, Aideen, and Orla, but we got away. And that whole reality is gone now, anyway. But yes, you did do all those things."

"I would never have killed you three," I said. "In my dreams, I fully intended to only stun you. I could never kill you, Dani. Nor could I kill Aideen. Orla, I never knew well, but I knew you loved her, and I wouldn't kill someone you love."

"We'll never know for sure, Charles. That reality is gone, and in this reality, James lived, but he died not long after, in a storm at sea."

"I'm sorry," I said.

"So that's your list of murder victims you want to save?" asked Dani. "There were no others?"

"There was Ciara's father," I said. "You remember that incident, of course."

"How could I forget," said Dani. "I still feel it was wrong for you to kill him, but Ciara is so tied up in all the events after that it would probably seriously change her future if you went back and saved him."

"I wouldn't save that scoundrel," I said. "He got what he deserved."

"You were wrong to kill him, Charles. You understand that, don't you?"

I'd had many years to reflect on all the murders I'd committed, and yes, I was wrong in every case. Murder was wrong, and I took the justification of self-defense way past its boundaries in all those cases. A madman has only insanity as a defense, and while I'm no lawyer, I feel sure I could have mounted a rigorous insanity defense had I ever been taken to court, but it's old news how I got out of that. More to the point, I was no longer insane and could think rationally about what I had done, and I was suffering terrible guilt over it.

"I do understand, Dani," I said. "And I very much want to right those wrongs."

"What would you do with the people if you actually were able to save them?" she asked.

"I'd bring them here, of course. That way, there would be no damage to the balance of time on Earth. Do you agree?"

"I suppose," said Dani. "But who knows, Charles. None of us really know how time travel affects reality."

"So true," I said. "But I'm committed to this course, Dani."

"And what if you succeed? What will your next mission be?"

"I don't know. But it will only be for good, I promise you that."

I meant what I said with all my heart, but Dani had a way of nudging me in the right direction that only one other person could come close to, her lover, Aideen. Those two knew how to get through to me and make sense of things that I couldn't see clearly. And in this case, Dani put her foot down once again.

"Charles, I'll support you on the missions to save the lives you took. But only if you promise me that you'll destroy the time station after that and never build another one."

I could have easily lied to get Dani's support. And frankly, I didn't need her support to do what I wanted with time travel. I didn't need anyone but myself for that. The issue of the time link could be overcome, but that wasn't a concern for me at that moment. The issue was honor. Integrity. I had been a liar for many years, but people can change. And regarding Dani and Aideen, two people who had accepted me as a friend despite so much wrongdoing, I would not risk losing them to get what I wanted.

"I'll agree to that, Dani. I promise you."

"Okay, so what next?" she asked.

"I don't need your help in the mission, Dani. I can do this on my own. But what I do need is time. Annette is meeting with Clarion and Zephyr tomorrow, and

I'm sure destroying my time station is at the top of her list. I haven't been invited to the meeting. Have you?"

"I have," said Dani. "How much can I tell them about what you want to do?"

"Nothing, I'm afraid. I'm sorry, but Annette won't approve of any form of time travel, no matter the cause. We're too far down the line for that."

"I suppose you're right," said Dani. "But I want to discuss this with Aideen. Do you have a problem with that?"

"Not at all. You two are my most trusted friends. But please, ask her not to say anything at the meeting. I'm assuming she's going too?"

"Yes, she is. And that's fine. We won't say anything."

"Can you tell me how much time I have after the meeting?"

"Okay," said Dani.

Chapter 6

Before I tell you what happened next, I want to remind you of what a beautiful place our settlement on Terrene had become. You will remember that the official name was Base One, but that is such a drastic understatement for what the land we had built from the depths of the ocean had become. I had been lobbying for the name "New Madagascar" to become the official name of our island. It was similar in size—around a thousand kilometers long and four hundred wide—and its shape was also very close to the island nation off the coast of eastern Africa. The similarities ended there because we had no mountains (although I could build mountains if so motivated), and the temperature was more moderate and far more stable. Still, we really needed to change that name!

There was always a light breeze, the sun shone 90 percent of the time, and we had farms and fields and forests that stretched over the whole island, dotted with freshwater lakes and crisscrossed with saltwater canals we had built to allow Water People to visit and spend time with us, until such time that the technology to convert their fins to legs was popularized. The temperature was a stable 21 degrees Celsius (70 Fahrenheit) during our fifteen daylight hours and only modestly lower at night. Some might say it was so perfect that it was boring, but we had plenty of adventure on Terrene. Around two or three times a year, we would notice the wind blowing harder than usual, which meant a giant wave was coming. The wind blew from east to west most of the time, so the eastern side of the island was where the waves usually hit. You will also remember that we built the island one thousand meters above sea level to protect us from these waves, which rarely exceeded five hundred meters in height.

But five hundred meters! On Earth, a wave of thirty meters in height is considered massive and extremely rare. There was some geological evidence that some seventy-five thousand years in the past, a colossal volcano collapsed into the sea off the western coast of Africa, and this produced a wave three hundred meters tall, but no one knows for sure, and even if someone had been alive to see it, it would pale in comparison to the waves we witness here on Terrene several times a year. It's not easy to describe such an extraordinary sight because these waves are taller than the once-famous Empire State Building and wider than the eye can see in both directions. The wave crashes against our island as a whale crashes into a minnow, hardly noticing it. After traveling along both our northern and southern coasts and leaving our island behind, the crest reforms in the area where our land temporarily blocked it, and the wave travels on until it is out of sight, eventually dying out when the wind subsides.

We also have an undersea world at our disposal, which is so vast it dwarfs the oceans of Earth. Not only is the planet 99% water, the surface area is double that of Earth, and the water is a hundred times deeper in places than the deepest oceans on Earth. True, we never venture below a depth of three thousand meters because we abide by the terms of our treaty with the Water People, who want to leave the revered creatures of the deep ocean alone, but there's plenty to see even so, and we have the Water People to show it to us. Later, I will tell you more of my growing relationship with Cabal, the leader of the Water People, but for now, I must conclude my report of the goings on when Annette visited Terrene to tear down my time station.

I had arranged for Dani and Aideen to visit me after the meeting. I understood quite clearly that those two were very close with Annette and I was confident they would have a private lunch with her after the official proceedings at the administrative offices where Clarion and Zephyr worked. I wondered if those two would be able to keep their promise to me, not telling Annette that I already knew what she wanted. I assumed they would ultimately spill the beans because I'd purposely given them an out, asking them only to not speak of my "inside information" at the official meeting. I was certain they would reveal the truth to Annette when the three of them were alone. And that was fine. It's what I wanted, actually. I wanted Annette to know she could keep no secrets from me any longer. I knew from a long history together that Dani and Aideen would inevitably become the mediators between Annette and me, as they had done many times before. That's also what I wanted. Those two were better at getting things from Annette than I ever was.

Dani and Aideen knocked on my door around 9 p.m., late afternoon on Terrene. But it wasn't just Dani and Aideen; Annette was with them. Can you imagine what I was feeling at the time? Betrayal, anger, fear? Yes, all of those and more. I had been having daydreams of a great, pitched battle, my home as the centerpiece of it all. In my fantasy, I had called upon the Land People to defend my time station from the invaders from Earth. They had come to me a thousand-fold and brought with them a portable force field to repel the guns of the platoon Annette had transported from Earth to attack my home and destroy my time station. Of course, we had prevailed, but now here she was, no army behind her, accompanied only by two of my closest friends. And then she reached out with her hand and touched me on the shoulder.

"I'm sorry to come unannounced, Charles," she said, her voice smooth and seductive, but it was working. I melted like chocolate on a hot day at the beach.

"Why are you here, Annette," I said, trying and failing to sound stern.

She smiled, and I liquified into a pathetic puddle of mush. Her hand was still on my shoulder.

"Charles, I was so touched by what you told Dani about wanting to go back and save the soldiers' lives, the ones you…."

"Murdered," I said, then broke down in tears. I turned away and went back into my home, my hand on my face, wiping away the moisture, embarrassed, humiliated, but also so moved that I didn't know how to handle it. Annette seemed so sincere. Was it true? Did she still have feelings for me? Did she care that I was a new person and wanted to right as many of my wrongs as possible? I needed to regain control, but it was so hard. A lifetime of shame and resentment just melted away with a touch to the shoulder and a kind word. What kind of a wimp had I become? I steeled myself and turned to face the three women.

"Excuse me, ladies," I said. "I'm just processing a lot at the moment. Please, come in. Join me for some coffee, will you?"

Dani stepped forward, taking over just when I needed someone to.

"Of course," she said. "Let's have some coffee and sit and talk. Just the four of us."

Chapter 7

We gathered at my kitchen table, I served coffee and pastries, and we talked. Annette had already breached the subject, so there was no need to dance around it. I had recovered from my emotional lapse. I was embarrassed, but the feeling of warmth I had received from Annette had not left me. I still had no idea, however, about Annette's intentions because her mind was cut off to me, as were the minds of Dani and Aideen. I assumed they were using the blocking feature of the multi-purpose device we all carried, nicknamed the "Handy," because it helped with so many of the day-to-day activities on Earth—paying for food and travel, making phone calls, sending entertainment of all forms directly to the brain, and allowing for telepathic communication. Apparently, it also worked, blocking my rudimentary mind-reading capability, but it didn't matter because the cat was out of the bag anyway, as I've said. I jumped right in, emboldened by Annette's small display of emotion toward me.

"Annette, I very much appreciate your feelings about my plan to travel back and attempt to save my…uh… victims. Does it mean you don't intend to try and stop me?"

Annette sat back in her chair, remaining quiet, as she often did when thinking, but Aideen stepped in and spoke first. I should take a moment to tell you just how far back I go with Aideen. You may recall that Aideen's mother, Aoife, conceived Aideen through artificial insemination—paid for with money I'd given her—when she was sixty-nine, having been made young by the pills from the future I'd also provided. Not long after her child was born, in 1954, I had the opportunity to meet baby Aideen, and I watched her grow into a beautiful young woman, seeing her once or twice a year during my travels through that time. At the age of eighteen, she became a time link herself, and I worked with her directly for the next fifty years.

I must admit that if there was ever going to be a woman to take my mind and heart off of Annette, it would have been Aideen. I found her fiery red hair and tall, lithe frame intoxicating and her inquisitive mind quite formidable. And while I would have been willing to go beyond the bounds of our professional relationship, my feelings were never reciprocated.

I had no idea of her sexual proclivities, and for all I know, neither did she, until one day, near the end days of the Time Chain I had built, she told me of a young woman named Dani, whom she'd fallen in love with and wanted to make a time link. And you know the rest of the story. Perhaps I'll talk about my feelings toward Dani at another time, but now I must return to my recounting of the fate of the time machine I had built on Terrene.

As I said, Aideen spoke first. "Charles, it is indeed a fine and noble thing you want to attempt, but if I may, I'd like to share with you some…food for thought, if you will."

"Very well," I said, always open-minded to others' opinions, especially those of Aideen and Dani.

"The three of us discussed the matter briefly on the way over," said Aideen, "and the thought has occurred to us that the soldiers you want to save will be very resistant to coming with you."

"You've guessed my plan then? To use a clone of myself as the time link, travel back to myself of the past, and bring the soldiers back here with me."

"When you told me you didn't need any help," said Dani, "I figured cloning was your only option. You need a time link to get you to those times and places, and if you're not seeking help, you would have no choice but to use a clone of yourself."

"But Charles," said Aideen. "The soldiers will not be responsive to the man they were sent to capture, no matter how persuasive you are with them."

"I could incapacitate them," he said. "Then bring them here without a fight. The Ticklers they carry won't hurt me, and the AI in my office uses that same tech, so it can't hurt me either."

"But wouldn't you want to give them a choice?" asked Annette. "I checked the records on those first four soldiers, and they had families. They wouldn't be happy here without them, and sending them back to Earth nearly seventy-five years after their deaths would be equally destabilizing, not only for them but for their families as well."

"I'm not so sure about that, Annette. I understand how living here would be difficult for them, but if you're willing to send them back to Earth, reuniting them with their families should be a good thing, not a bad thing. And why wouldn't we simply let them rejoin their families in their present rather than today's present."

The room went silent, and I wondered where this discussion would end. I couldn't tell if Annette would support me or not, and I sensed there was something they had yet to bring up that might turn the tide against me, and I was right. It was Dani who revealed the blatant flaw in my plan.

"Charles," she said. "Let's say you make it back here with the four soldiers you killed in 2185 and the two you killed in 1801. And then we take them back to Earth and reunite them with their families as if they hadn't been killed that day, and everyone is happy. Mission accomplished?"

It all sounded good, but something told me I was being set up. Nevertheless, I responded with my true feelings. "Absolutely. Couldn't ask for a better result."

"And your clone?" asked Dani, bludgeoning me with the weak link of the entire operation.

"What of it?" I asked, pretending not to know where this was headed.

"You can't live on the same planet with your clone, Charles," said Aideen. "So what would you do with him?"

You may recall that the cloning technology of the Land People created an exact duplicate of the original, in every way, including not only physical replication but mental and emotional. The problem was that if allowed to live together on the same planet, the clone and the original would be inside each other's heads the entire time, living two lives and ultimately going insane and killing themselves. The Land People had confirmed that this exact thing had happened repeatedly in the early days of cloning, so they adopted a new policy: to create a clone only when the individual was nearing death. In more recent times, when the clone of Aideen was made, she was sent to Earth, 737 light years away from Terrene, so the two could live without ruining each other's lives. With that in mind, I had a quick answer to Aideen's question.

"We send him to Earth, of course," I said. The truth is that this was a lie. After all, I knew my identical self would not be legally permitted to live on Earth because I had been banished from Earth in perpetuity due to the crimes I had committed there. But I threw it out there, demanding equal treatment. "Just as you did with your clone, Aideen."

The room fell silent again, and I knew in my heart they all had guessed my true intention regarding my clone. The paradox of my plan to save the people I had murdered was that I would need to murder my clone when the mission was completed. Annette put words to the dilemma I faced, which further boxed me in.

"Earth law is clear," she said. "A clone has the same rights as any human being."

Meaning you could not simply murder a clone and walk away. On Earth.

"Earth law doesn't apply here on Terrene," I countered.

"It does now," said Annette. "A referendum was taken this morning of all residents of Terrene to adopt the laws of Earth here. Cabal was also here and had no objection to the laws applying to all land on Terrene, but making it clear that the Laws of the Sea would still govern the oceans."

"That couldn't be," I said. "I wasn't contacted regarding any such thing."

"You may cast your vote now," said Annette. "Just so you know, it won't change anything. The vote was unanimously in favor of adopting the laws of Earth, among both Land People and humans."

Again, silence ruled the room. I must admit that while the encounter with Annette had begun with such warmth for me, my blood was now running cold, knowing that Annette had once again outmaneuvered me. But I had one more arrow in my quiver, and I unleased it at that moment. "Would you be willing to function as my time link, Annette, to help me save the four soldiers? After all, you and I were working together then, remember?"

Surprisingly, Annette seemed prepared for this possibility. "Charles, we all want to help you, and if we could, we would want to help those poor soldiers too. But time travel was made illegal on Earth because of how it affects the balance of time. We've all lived our lives for seventy-five years, during which those four soldiers were not alive. By bringing them back, we cannot know what that means for any of us. What will change? Who knows? And that is why time travel is illegal on Earth, and now, on Terrene. No citizen can use time travel. I am not above the law, Charles."

"But what about the Executive Committee?" I pleaded. "They've approved exceptions for you before. Why not now, when lives could be saved?"

Annette reached for me again and touched my shoulder, and I was her prisoner once again. "My dear Charles," she said. "My mind and heart tell me that too much is at risk to pursue your idea. But it has not gone without my most sincere appreciation, and that of Aideen and Dani, that this is so important to you. Somehow, however, you must live with it. And I believe you know in your heart that it would be wrong to take your clone's life to save those soldiers. Will you work with me, Charles? I sincerely have your best interests in mind."

Chapter 8

After the meeting with Annette, Dani, and Aideen, I allowed the time station to be destroyed without a fight. In the end, Annette was right, and I couldn't resist her desires anyway. And while neither of the three had used the word "murderer" during our conversation, there was no doubt that is what I was. What I am. And I'd proven it, once again, by my willingness to murder my clone. I wondered if that meant I would still murder others if my self-interest was at stake, and while I didn't know the answer, I suspected it was probably, yes.

The irony of the destruction of my time station was that everyone involved knew I could build another one if I chose to, but that didn't matter. Annette could go back to Earth and report she had not only successfully destroyed the time station but also brought Terrene to heal by placing it under the jurisdiction of Earth, once and for all. There was one massive exception to that agreement, however, one that I felt I should turn my attention to—the Water People. As expected, Cabal had insisted that the Laws of the Sea remain the sole guiding principles of life in the oceans of Terrene. To the Water People, the three Laws of the Sea were all that mattered, and if any ambiguity between the laws of Earth and the Laws of the Sea ever surfaced, the one billion Water People would undoubtedly fight to make sure the Laws of the Sea prevailed. But that was an issue for another day and not likely to ever be a problem anyway since the laws of Earth were highly compatible with the Terrene Laws of the Sea: take no more than you need, do not pollute, and do not disturb the creatures of the deep.

None of this mattered to me. The events leading to the destruction of my time station had simply pointed me in a direction. It wasn't as if I intended to exact my revenge on Earth in general, and Annette in particular, for bringing Terrene into the fold and destroying my time station. Once I got over the humiliation of once again being outsmarted by Annette while still trying to maintain my commitment to doing good things, it was really a happy coincidence that the Water People were not bound by the laws of Earth. It felt good to know there was a place on Terrene I could still go and be completely free of the shackles of Earth, but in the end, my reason for deciding to venture into the sea was to feed my unending curiosity to learn and experience things I had not yet fully explored. Where this might lead, only time would tell.

I resolved that when I went under the water, I would not return for some time. I don't know why this was, but I thought that somewhere inside me was a desire to send a message to those who had wronged me by taking my rights away. Yes, it was about Annette, primarily, and to some extent, Dani and Aideen, who had colluded with her to seize and destroy my time station. Here is my logic: Before Annette made her diplomatic visit to Terrene, I was free to build and use my time station, but by the time she left, I was not. I had stated, proven actually, that my only intent for the machine was to do good, and when I sent Dani and the cloning techs back to clone an Aideen that was three years in the past, so she could be matched with a Dani that had appeared from some false reality, also three years younger, I had done it for them. By the way, I need to tell you, at some point, what happened to Danielle and the clone of Aideen back on Earth, but since that was later, I'll save it until then. Best to tell a story in the order it happened.

Therefore, back to my story of losing my freedom. Because Annette had imposed the laws of Earth on Terrene, when I asked to be given a chance to right my own wrongs, I was denied that opportunity. True, I hadn't worked it out completely, but there would have been ways to do it without the need for the clone, for example, if Annette had permitted me to use the new time travel tech housed in her building on Earth, but that offer had not been forthcoming. Instead, they changed the laws of Terrene, and my hope of rectifying my horrifying wrongs was callously ripped away from me. Now, I was left with nothing but the sea to help me vent my anger and pursue my unquenchable thirst for more.

Regarding my pending undersea adventure, you must know me well enough to realize that I wasn't just going to dive in and swim around, saying hi to all the creatures lurking under there. Of course not. I had a plan, and you will learn what it was soon enough. But there was another benefit to going under the sea for a long time; a message, if you will; a message that would ultimately get through to Annette, and that was simply this: "You can't stop me when I'm down here."

Chapter 9

Before I went under the water, I made a preliminary visit to see Cabal, on the pontoon city he had built nearby, beseeching him to allow me to spend more time with him and his people. I realized Cabal didn't trust me in the way he trusted Dani and Aideen because he knew of my past, but he was also well aware of my recent string of heroic events here on Terrene. I not only had done much good here for the people of all species, but I had also demonstrated that I had power. And power was something that a powerful man like Cabal respected. He granted my request, telling me to come whenever I was ready and that he and his people would accept me with open arms.

I returned to New Madagascar (I'm calling it that, and I don't care what other people call it.) and began my preparations. I didn't want to visit in the same manner Dani and Aideen had done, housing themselves in the air aquarium and making day trips with Cabal to see the sights. I wanted to live as one of the Water People, swimming and living and pissing and shitting in the water, just as they did. To do that would take some effort, but because of my unique intelligence and special abilities, it wouldn't be insurmountable and very likely would be the envy of all who lived on the land when my latest invention was complete.

I envisioned a skinsuit that turned my legs into a powerful tailfin and covered my head with an enclosure that would keep the water out but still absorb the water's oxygen and bring it into my lungs through my mouth and nose. It would be designed to filter waste like the skintight clothing of the Land People filtered it, recycling the water and nutrients and expelling the rest as an inert gas. Technically, this gas would be my "shit and piss"; it just wouldn't smell bad. I wondered if Water People could smell, anyway. The suit would also be highly resistant to cold temperatures and the intense atmospheric pressure of the depths. It would need to withstand three hundred atmospheres at three thousand meters—the self-imposed depth limit of the Water People— but my suit would take much more pressure than that because part of my plan was to venture further down if I could talk Cabal into it. No small task since going deeper would violate the third law of the sea, but we would see if there were ways to work around that.

When my suit was done and thoroughly tested, I wanted to spend time with my friends, especially Dani and Aideen, before leaving. I arranged to meet those two at Murphy's, knowing that Liam and Orla would be there since they not only worked there, they lived upstairs. I also asked Clarion and Zephyr to come, pulling together my list of attendees for my unofficial going-away party. I sidled up to the bar to speak with Liam and Orla before the other guests arrived, and when they did, I suggested we have a seat at one of the round tables for six. Orla joined us, leaving Liam at the bar, but he wasn't offended. Liam understood me, wanted only the best for me, and would never begrudge me the chance to be with our other friends before leaving.

Of all my friends on Terrene, Liam was my closest. It was hard to refer to him as my best friend, but it would be him if I had a best friend. He had known me when I was at my worst, even when I had imprisoned old Orla in the time chamber I built below his cottage. But he didn't love Orla then, not the old woman she'd become. He loved the young girl of twelve he'd met fifty-four years ago. I wasn't sure he even knew the stooped old hag I'd tied to a time cradle was her, especially since he was inebriated during most of his waking hours. But it didn't matter. Liam was a man of adventure, and he'd never encountered another human being with more adventures up his sleeve than me. After all, without me, this whole new life he'd built on Terrene would not have been possible, and he knew it. But he would have been my friend, even if we were still on Earth. So it was with the confidence of a best friend that Liam smiled when we left the bar to sit at a table in his pub. He knew he would see me again.

We all ordered ale, and Aideen raised her glass. "To Charles! May he conquer the oceans as he has conquered the land."

"TO CHARLES," came the call of the table and the surrounding tables too. I was well known on Terrene, as you already know.

Not to be outdone, Dani tempered Aideen's toast. "Please, Charles, don't take that literally, okay? I mean, we like Cabal too!"

Everyone laughed, realizing perhaps that if I wanted to, I could conquer the sea, but I didn't want that. I wanted to experience it, not only the life under the water but the legends I'd heard whispers of from Cabal himself. "I won't take it literally," I promised. "I just want to learn more about the way of things under the water, and after the stories you and Aideen told of your 'Thirty Days Under the Sea,' I can't resist trying something similar.

"How long will you be under, Charles?" asked Aideen.

"A long while, I hope," I replied. "Longer than thirty days, I would think."

"It's not a record you need to break, Charles," said Aideen. "We only stayed that long because circumstances forced us to."

"Going to miss me then, lass, are you now?" I said, doing my best imitation of an Irish accent.

"Indeed," said Aideen. "We all will."

I have heard you invented a suit that will let you live under the water almost as easily as we live up here on the land, said Zephyr. *Is it true?*

"Why yes, it is," I said, happy to have some interest shown already in my latest miraculous invention.

We would very much like to try a suit like that one day, said Zephyr.

"I promise you, then, that you will," I responded. "When I return."

After an hour or so, Clarion and Zephyr begged off, saying they needed to return to work, and Orla went back up to the bar to be with Liam, leaving me alone with Aideen and Dani. I was happy about that because I wanted to ask them a question I wasn't comfortable sharing with the others.

"How was the visit from Annette, from your perspective, ladies?" I asked.

"Was great to see her," said Aideen. "She's a wonderful person, Charles, if you didn't know."

"Yes, yes, of course," I said. "But you two are well aware that Annette and I have a complicated history. And it does get old being outfoxed by her, time and time again. Of course, aided and abetted by you two."

I smiled, trying to lighten the moment, but Dani wasn't buying it. "Are you still angry about the time station, Charles? Is that why you're leaving us?"

"I'm not leaving," I said, somewhat defensively. "I'm exploring."

"You can explore without going under the water for months at a time," said Aideen.

"I don't understand why you're trying to talk me out this Aideen. Can you please explain?"

"Everyone on Base One will miss ya' Charles. You're an essential part of our community. But most of those people don't know ya' like Dani and I do. We know you've got mischief on your mind, Charles, and the more time you stay under the water, the more likely you'll end up doin' somethin' you'll regret. Better to just stay up here with us."

Aideen had a point. And while I wasn't certain myself precisely what I'd be doing under the water, it wasn't lost on me, or on Aideen and Dani, that my motivation stemmed from agitation at being outsmarted by Annette and my desire to be free of the laws she'd put in place here on New Madagascar. But it was good to receive some sound, straightforward advice from Aideen and Dani that might help me to stay out of trouble.

"I appreciate your concern, ladies, truly," I said. "And it helps me to be reminded of my tendencies toward the dark side, but I assure you, I will keep all of that under control. After all, I've been a good boy for a while here, and I want to keep my stellar record intact. It's important to me to stay on the good side."

"Very well, then," said Aideen, a suspicious expression on her face.

"And you'll be leaving yourselves soon, won't you," I said. "For your tour on Earth."

It was the middle of 2257 by then, July on Earth, and Dani and Aideen were scheduled to go back there in three or four months when their one-year tour on Terrene ended. They would be replaced by the other Dani and Aideen, the ones that were three years younger, and I really wasn't that enthusiastic about the change. I thought of these two as the real Dani and Aideen and the other two as, well, less than real. I wondered if others felt the same way.

"How are those two doing back on Earth?" I asked.

There was a pause, but then Dani answered. "Not well, if you must know," she said.

"Why?" I asked. "What's wrong."

"Annette tells me they feel out of place," she said. Aideen's clone is struggling with the time gap between her last experience and the present, and the other Dani feels disconnected in some way she can't explain. They've been released and are living in the apartment Aideen and I rented, with our permission, but I can't say it's been smooth sailing for them. My parents have even sent messages saying they're concerned and don't seem to be able to help. So things are a bit out of sync, I'd say, for the other two of us."

"I'm terribly sorry to hear that, Dani. I hope things improve, truly. And what of Annette? I didn't spend much time with her when she was here. Admittedly, it was my fault. I simply struggle to be comfortable around her."

"That's a shame," said Dani. "She cares for you, Charles."

"Does she?" I asked, and I wanted to know more. "What leads you to believe that, Dani?"

"Well, you know she's a very private person," said Dani. "But you're not as reserved about your past, and you told us once that you and Annette were together at one time. So we know that, and we can piece that together with some of her comments…."

"Like what?" I asked, thirsting for any tidbit that might inform me of Annette's feelings for me.

"She has asked us, several times, back on Earth and here, how you are doing. And not just casually. She really wants to know if you're like your old self, the one she knew way back when."

"Do you think she forgives me for all I have done?" I asked, hopeful, and Aideen stepped back into the conversation.

"Forgiveness is a big word, in this case, wouldn't you agree, Charles? After all, Annette's only human. All of us are. You did some really terrible things."

"I did," I said, lowering my head. "And why should I expect others to forgive me when I can't even forgive myself?"

"You shouldn't, Charles," said Aideen. "That's the point."

"But it doesn't mean people can't love you, Charles, despite your wrongdoing," said Dani.

With that comment, I lost my ability to speak. To think that people, such as the two sitting at the table with me at that moment, and the other two up at the bar, and maybe Clarion and Zephyr, and perhaps even Annette Li, might love me, was too much for me to bear.

Dani could see I was emotionally distraught and reached over and put her hand on top of mine. It helped. And when I'd settled down, I considered the possibility that I wasn't yet ready to ask for the love of anyone because I had yet to learn how to truly love myself.

Chapter 10

The underwater skinsuit worked well. I wasn't as fast of a swimmer as the Water People, but I was much faster than a human would be, even if they were using fins. Cabal gave me a cave of my own to live in, nestled in amongst one of the living areas occupied by his people. I learned to cook the way they did it, but I also used a grinder to pulverize the food into a mush that I would then put into a squeeze bottle. I could open the skinsuit anywhere I wanted, using commands from my brain, just as my brain would tell my mouth to open and close or give any other bodily command. To eat, I would open the skinsuit covering my mouth, insert the tube of food, close my lips around it, and squeeze, all while keeping the skinsuit closed over my nostrils so I could breathe through my nose. Over time, I got good at eating this way.

I met all the neighbors and found them timid at first, but they slowly opened up to me after they realized I wasn't so different from them. A little boy lived in the family next door who seemed both fascinated and terrified of me. He was less than half the length of a full-grown Water Person, around one meter long, but I had no idea how old he was. On my first day living in my cave, I noticed him peering into my living quarters from the side he lived in. The entrances to all caves were open, as if privacy wasn't a priority for the Water People, and I wondered if it was because they didn't have sex like humans do. On Earth, most female fish release their eggs into the water, and the eggs are then fertilized by the males. Sharks and rays use a form of penetration to reproduce, but it's not like they mate for life. On the contrary, male sharks mate as often as possible with any female shark nearby.

So in the fish world on Earth, nobody really knew who their kids were. But the Water People weren't really fish. They had family units similar to humans, and they bore a limited number of children throughout their lives. I don't know how many, but from what I could see, there were usually two or three of the young ones living in any given cave. And I found out soon enough that they mate similarly to humans as well, just without the preconceived notion that these activities should be carried out in private. I saw it happening as I swam by peoples' homes fairly frequently.

Anyway, back to the little boy. The first day I moved in, I could see his little hands grasping the corner of my cave front, and then I saw his little face slowly come into view, and I sensed fear in him. So I smiled and waved, and he darted away and back into his cave. He went through this regimen several times a day, and one day I was able to hold him in place by offering him a shrimp, a favorite snack of the Water People. I edged up to him, holding out the shrimp, and when I got close enough, he snatched it from me and stuffed it into his mouth, using his sharp teeth to munch it up and swallow it down. Eventually, I was able to lure him into my cave by offering more shrimp, and as time went by, we became fast friends.

His name was Gilamead, and he was good company for me during the time I spent in the cave. He taught me how to play a game the children played out in the passageways called Skiff. It was played with a disk-like device, some kind of shell from another underwater species, that was heavy enough and flat enough to fly through the water as a frisbee did on old Earth. There was a team sport centered around the Skiff, which I never played, but Gilamead and I played catch for hour upon hour, and he always seemed to be proud of it. I got to know his parents as well, and they often invited me over for dinner, much to the delight of my young friend.

We communicated telepathically, and it was good practice. I'd been communicating back and forth with the Land People that way for some time but didn't get to do it very often since most of my contact with them was at Murphy's, and it made the humans who were inevitably present uncomfortable when I spoke in that manner. All of them could do it as well, using their handys, but there was an unwritten rule at Murphy's that humans should do everything the old-fashioned way, in keeping with Liam's original reasoning for coming to Terrene and building his pub.

I didn't see Cabal during my first few weeks underwater, and I wondered if he was avoiding me because he didn't care for me or for other reasons. As I look back on my time living in his world, I realize he wanted me to get to know his people on a personal level before he inserted himself into my life. It's clear to me now that the reticence of his people early in my stay had as much to do with them being intimated by Cabal, the great leader of their world, as it did with their unfamiliarity with me. By staying away early on, Cabal was doing me a favor, and it helped me to get a real taste of what it was like to be one of the Water People and to actually become friends with them.

We lived around one thousand meters below the surface, and it was quite dark at that depth, but the Water People had more than eyes to show them around. Like many underwater species on Earth, they were equipped with echolocation glands that enabled them to see in the dark, especially for hunting. I had a mechanical echolocation device embedded in my skinsuit, so I could go hunting with them, but I never caught anything. I hadn't brought any weaponry, such as a speargun, which would help me hunt, primarily because I was fearful I might accidentally shoot a Water Person, which would not go over well. I was simply too slow to catch anything worth eating, so I relied on the generosity of the Water People when it came to my food.

There was one underwater species, some kind of fish-like creature, that was about one meter long and would have looked very much like a fish from Earth, a tuna perhaps, except it had two heads, one on each end. With no rear fin for propulsion, you would think the thing would be a slow swimmer, and it was slower than most of the other animals I encountered down there. But its ability to swim in two directions made it a difficult target. I would gain on it, and just as I was about to grab it with my hands, it would come to an abrupt halt and slide right under me, heading in the opposite direction. Anyway, this species was known as Spawn among the Water People, and while the word was unrelated to the English word, the Spawn in the waters of Terrene was a food staple, at least it was in the area of that ocean where I was living. The preparation was simple: cut off both heads, gut the fish, filet it, and poach it in the pressure ovens that every home was equipped with. The animal had no bones, so it was easy to eat, with no worry of choking to death on an unseen fishbone. Its meat was dark, but it had a good taste, something like swordfish.

The caves in which we lived, inside a mountain, had lights, as did the numerous passageways crisscrossing the interior of the residential areas. The outside entrances to the living areas were steel doors, similar to the one I had seen that blocked the entrance to the air aquarium. I found it ironic that they could be opened by pressing a code into an instrument panel, like a garage door of old on Earth, which I had seen many times during my travels to the past. I wondered why the doors were needed since it seemed like all the undersea life at these depths kept their distance from the Water People. It was as if they had removed themselves from the food chain, entitled to hunt other species but not to be hunted without consequences. This felt a little unfair to me at first, and it must not have been a hard and fast, never violated rule because the steel doors remained shut whenever they weren't being used for entry and exit.

Massive predators were living at these relatively shallow depths, like the twenty-meter-long shark-like beasts with three mouths—one at the front, one on the bottom, and one on the top. I saw them often, and yet they never even acknowledged my existence, and this told me that because I was with the Water People, I was also exempted from the food chain. I did make a note, however, not to go out swimming alone.

I longed to gain more knowledge of the deep, to see the monsters which supposedly ruled the bottom of the ocean. But I would need Cabal's permission and help to ever see the bottom and all that lived there. And after many weeks of living on my own, he finally made an appearance. And believe it or not, we did end up going to the bottom of the ocean, just not for the reasons I had wanted to go there in the first place.

Chapter 11

You will come to my home, Cabal insisted, when he visited me in my cave for the first time.
It would be my honor, was my response.
We left my mountain residence, and I noticed Cabal had come on a motorized vehicle, which surprised me. I had always considered him a free-swimming type, shunning the more modern technology, but my preconceived notions were obviously wrong.
It's a long way, he said. *We need this vessel to shorten our journey.*
As you say, sir, I replied.
We boarded the vessel, which was an open-top, meaning we would ride on the top of it, and the water would flow over us. Cabal told me to hold on tightly, and then the ship launched itself at high speed and ascended toward the light. I squeezed the hold handles with all my strength and pressed my feet up against the foot stops, (which had very like-

ly been placed there specifically for me) as we continued to accelerate. I would estimate our top speed reached eighty kilometers per hour, so to say it was a challenge to hold on was an understatement. I marveled at the strength of Cabal's arms because he had no feet to press against a foot stop, and he was driving with one arm and holding on with the other. His head was up, and he could see all around us, but I dared not keep my head up for long for fear of my neck breaking. Suffice it to say, I saw few sights along the way.

After five grueling hours of traveling this way, our vessel began to slow down and descend from the light-infused water back into the dark depths. I'd equipped my suit with a gauge that measured depth, temperature, and pressure, and of course, as the depth and pressure increased, the temperature decreased. At a depth of three thousand meters, it was pure black around me. The vessel slowed to a near stop, and I saw lights ahead. A door rose directly in front of us. We entered a vast, well-lit chamber filled with numerous other underwater ships.

We will change vessels here, said Cabal. *Please follow me.*

We slipped off the deck of our open-top vehicle and swam toward a much more substantial ship shaped like a classic submarine. It was around twenty meters long and four meters high. We entered through an open hatchway and went into the sub, which was full of water. There were only a few lights inside, but I could tell this was a serious deep-water craft. The ribbing that supported the hull's sides was tall and thick and spaced closely together. I felt as if I'd entered the bowels of a mutant whale, its exaggerated ribcage surrounding me as would the bars of an inescapable jail and giving the whale the strength to resist the tremendous pressures of even the deepest trenches of the ocean. There were numerous thick, round windows through which the outside world could be viewed and a substantial front window. There wasn't much to see now other than what I'd already seen—dozens of ships of different sizes—but anticipation filled my being regarding what I might witness after we departed the underwater base. At the moment, we were too deep to see anything other than what the headlights revealed, but it was still exciting. Perhaps we would go even deeper, and my wish to see the mythical beasts of the depths would be fulfilled.

    Most of the inside light was coming from the front of the ship, and I could see two Water People up there, floating in a horizontal position and working with instruments. I assumed they were the pilots, and Cabal confirmed as much. *These are my two most trusted pi-*

lots, he said. *They will take us on many voyages together if that is the will of the Watcher.*

I'd heard about the Watcher from the Sky from Dani and Aideen, and I knew that Cabal took it very seriously. I never heard much talk about the Watcher from the Water People living in my residence, so I can't really comment on the breadth of this faith throughout the Water People population. Still, I knew for Cabal, it was serious business. I nodded my head slowly, as if in reverence, and made a note to be very careful never to disparage Cabal's God in any way.

The vessel turned and exited through the same opening we had transited to enter the base. As our tail cleared the exit, I looked behind and saw the doors moving inexorably downward. The light extinguished as the door clanged shut, its closure echoing through the vessel's hull. We picked up speed gradually but continuously, and the world began racing by so fast there wasn't much to see, even with the headlights showing the way. For some reason, hanging there in the water-filled craft, I didn't feel our acceleration. *How fast are we going?* I asked Cabal, chastising myself for not incorporating a speedometer into my suit. Of course, I could do that next time, if there was a next time.

Around five hundred of your kilometers per hour, he replied. *You may sit if you like. The seats are designed* for our people, but since you are now shaped more like us, they should be fine for you.

Thank you, I said, arranging myself in one of the long curved seats and fastening the harness that would hold me in place. *How far is your home from here?*

Around nine hours at this speed.

I made the calculations, estimating that wherever we were going was nearly five thousand kilometers from where we had started. This was a relatively short distance for a planet with a circumference of seventy thousand kilometers at the equator, but our destination was a long way from New Madagascar. I wondered if our peace negotiations would have gone as smoothly if, by chance, our building operation had taken place right next door to Cabal's home.

Would you like some nourishment? asked Cabal.

I am hungry and thirsty, I replied. *But I didn't bring my feeding apparatus.*

Not a problem, said Cabal. *We will lower the water level in the vessel and pump air in. Since I can breathe in both water and air, I can join you.*

Cabal gave a command to the pilots, and the water level in the vessel lowered until it came down to my shoulders. The pilots were still underwater, but Cabal took a seat opposite me. He was around my height, so we were basically eye to eye. There was a table under the water, and Cabal had placed some food on it. I could see through the clear water that it was Spawn, and balls of fruit, which I had enjoyed before.

Do you mind eating with your hands? he asked. *I realize this is poor manners in your culture, but it doesn't matter in ours.*

Absolutely no problem, I replied, my stomach gurgling with hunger spasms.

Please, will you indulge me by allowing a small prayer before we eat?

Yes, certainly, I said, so famished and thirsty, I thought I might faint.

Cabal raised his hands into the air and turned his face skyward, and I imitated his gestures. His eyes were open, so I kept mine open as well, the ceiling of the vessel a few meters above my head.

Oh great Watcher from the Sky, hear me now. Today I will bring a Human to the great city you built for us many eons ago. He is the first outsider of any foreign species ever allowed within our gates. I pray that you accept my decision. I believe this Human can help our people come closer to you. That is my only intent, as always. Thank you also for the food we eat. May the bounty from the sea be forever clean and fresh.

Well, that was news. I didn't understand at all how I was going to help the Water People come closer to their God, but my curiosity was definitely peaked.

Chapter 12

As our journey to Cabal's home continued—which apparently was a great city of some sort, built by the Watcher from the Sky—we began to ascend. We leveled off only two hundred meters from the surface. There was plenty of light at this depth, at least much more than the pitch black enshrouding us most of the way, and I had a good view through the front windshield of what was ahead. Coming into view was an amazing sight: Three great pyramids sat on a plateau that rested at the same depth we were traveling at. The pyramids rose up toward the surface, nearly touching it, from what I could tell. Of course, I've been to the Necropolis at Giza many times, and while being underwater was a little disorienting, it looked as if these three structures were strikingly similar in height and positioning to the three pyramids at Giza, but that was where the similarities ended.

These three structures were made of clear glass or some other kind of transparent material. Inside, they were filled with seawater and hundreds, maybe thousands of Water People engaged in various activities. In one area, welders were building underwater ships. In another area, household items such as pots and pans were being formed, and in another, dozens of cooks worked at huge stoves and ovens, preparing food as if for a royal wedding. Other areas were blocked from view by darkened glass inside the structures, and I wondered what might be going on in those secret spots. The top floor of each structure was a mini-pyramid, and in one of them, slightly taller than the other two, was a throne room, very likely the place where Cabal sat and ruled. One of the other top floors contained a ballroom of sorts for grand celebrations and parties, perhaps. And the other one's top was of the darkened glass I'd seen in different sections, so I couldn't tell what went on there.

The submarine entered an opening around fifty meters below the plateau's surface and maneuvered its way through lighted passageways until it docked. The pilots remained in their seats, but Cabal got up. *Follow me, please,* he said.

We left the sub and swam horizontally for a dozen meters or so, entering a smaller tunnel, also well-lit, and then above us, I saw a vertical tunnel come into view. Cabal swam upward, and I followed him. After around fifty meters, we emerged into one of the pyramids. Inside, it seemed different from the outside, more like an office building than not, but as we swam higher, it opened up, and then we came up through an opening in the top floor, and I could see that we had entered the throne room. The Water People inside looked to be primarily soldiers, although they were dressed no differently than the others, meaning they paraded around entirely unclothed, as did all Water People. The only thing that caused me to think they were soldiers was that each of them had some kind of weapon held at their waist by a belt and a holster. Guns. The guards bowed as we passed by, and Cabal swam up to his throne and sat. There was a chair on each side of his throne, and he beckoned me to take one of them, which I did with haste, caught up in the vagaries of this whole royalty under the sea thing, my head swiveling around to take it all in.

As I sat, I looked around and saw that the hall was a great chamber that could comfortably hold several hundred Water People, and I wondered if such occasions came about with regularity. But for now, the place was empty, save for a dozen or so soldiers. The view out through the glass was crystal clear, but there was no sea life in my field of vision, and I wondered if being that close to the royal palace was prohibited. Very likely.

Soon we can talk, said Cabal. *But now you must witness something I think you will enjoy.*

Without further ado, I felt a gentle lurch, and the entire pyramid began to rise. Looking out through the glass, I could see the other two structures rising with us, slowly but surely reaching for the surface. Can you imagine what it was like when the apex of the pyramid in which we were sitting pierced the surface of the ocean and continued rising, like a massive ship emerging from the depths, water swirling down the angled glass sides and waves cresting out from their wake as if breaking on the shore of a beach? Up and up we went until it seemed we were well over a hundred meters above the surface, a fact I verified on my depth finder, which worked at all altitudes, both below and above the water. And then the relentless, ponderous rise ended, and we came to rest.

I peered out at the endless sea, nothing but water in all directions, until I looked north, and there I saw, in the distance, white land. Ice, actually. Cabal explained.

Our city, which is called Mirandia, sits far north of the equator, not far from the ice sheets of the northern pole. When the refreezing of the poles is completed, the ice sheets will cover us, but we will generate heat to keep the water above us liquid, so our opportunities to rise above the sea continue.

How long will we stay up here? I asked.

As long as we like, he replied.

Is this place known by the Land People? I asked.

No. It is a secret place known only to our people.

But couldn't they see it with the scopes on their space vessels? Their scope technology is very advanced.

This city serves two great purposes. One is to function as an antenna to the heavens, so the Watcher from the Sky can send instructions. The second purpose is to create a mirage for all who would pry into the business of the Watcher. The city emits an undiscoverable signal, covering a radius of around ten thousand of your meters, with the city at the center of the circle. The signal creates a mirage that blankets not only that entire area but travels all the way down to the very bottom of this great sea.

And what is the mirage, if I may be so bold as to ask?

The mirage is of the ocean, which is what the scopes of Land People see when they look down upon this area. Only ocean.

Forgive me, Cabal, if I am mistaken. But I spoke at length with Dani and Aideen about their time under the water with you, and not only did they not mention this place, but they also said you claimed to have been given no technology by the Watcher from the Sky.

Yes, I said that, he replied. *It was a lie. We have this sacred city, given to us by the Watcher.*

You also told Dani that the Watcher had never come to the surface of Terrene.

That is true, said Cabal. *Only the Emissaries of the Watcher have visited Terrene.*

I don't understand, I said.

I will show you all that I know. And then, perhaps, the Watcher will reward us both.

Chapter 13

Cabal told me we would be leaving immediately for a critical mission related to our recent discussion but would return later. I followed him back through his pyramid-shaped palace and down into the bowels of the rock below, negotiating the network of passages until we found and boarded his deep-water submarine. I remind you that all of this time, all of my time under the water, in fact, I had been completely submerged in it (other than the brief moment when Cabal had lowered the water level in the sub, so I could eat). You must realize that for a human to be not only living underwater but living in the water itself was another first for me. I don't believe any other human has done this before. I'm not really bragging (well, a little, I suppose, you know I can't help myself!), but what's more important for you to understand is how very different it was than just strolling along in an atmosphere of clean air, as were all of my friends up above, at that very moment. At first, it was like having claustrophobia, especially living in that small cave, but as time went by, it became tolerable. As with anything, practice makes perfect, and I was getting better at being a fish as time passed.

Anyway, we entered the sub and set off on our next "mission," but where we were going was a mystery to me since Cabal hadn't provided details. The pilots were still upfront as if they'd never left.

Please sit and strap yourself in, said Cabal.

I did as he asked, and he did the same, sitting beside me this time rather than across from me.

Where are we going, Cabal?

We are going down, he replied. *To the great depths you so very much wanted to see.*

But I thought that was against the third law of the sea.

There are exceptions, he said. *For me. When I have business to conduct there.*

What business? I asked.

I want to introduce you to someone you should know.

Who?

You will see, he replied.

The sub maneuvered deftly through the network of tunnels and entered a cavern. It was circular, shaped like a cylinder, and about fifty meters wide. The submarine slowly turned its nose downward, ultimately ending up completely vertical. I fell forward into the straps and almost wished I'd sat on the other side of the table, but then I would have missed whatever lay ahead of us. Then the sub dove. I saw the opening of a vertical tunnel, around ten meters in diameter, looming in front of us. We entered, and soon there were no lights, and all became perfectly black in front of me. Nothing to see. The sub's lights switched on, and I could see lifeforms of various sizes and shapes, most of them clinging to the walls, a few in the more central waters, but moving quickly aside to avoid being crushed by the fast-moving sub.

We didn't go as fast as we had in open water, which was understandable since there were only a few meters between the sub and the rock walls of the tunnel. I estimated our speed at around forty kilometers per hour, but I really had no idea how fast we were going since the close proximity to the walls of the tunnel, speeding by tremendously fast, caused my perception to be distorted. We continued this way for over an hour, finally slowing our descent when we were over fifty thousand meters below the surface. That's fifty kilometers, my friends. The deepest waters on Earth are barely eleven kilometers deep. I remembered from our initial surveys that the waters near the equator were up to eighty kilometers deep, but the depths as one approached the poles became less, so I suspected we were nearing the bottom. Just then, my suspicion was confirmed as the sub began to turn back to a horizontal position, slowing and inching toward an opening in the wall. Another tunnel.

We entered the horizontal tunnel and traveled at low speed for about ten minutes, and then we emerged from the rock altogether. In front of me, spread out on the ocean floor, I saw what looked like a city of lights, hundreds of them. As we approached, I noticed that each light was shaped somewhat like an egg, except the side that sat on the bottom was flat. They varied in size, the smallest being only about one meter tall and half a meter in diameter at the wide point. The largest I estimated to be ten meters tall and five meters wide. They all looked quite sturdy and would have to be at this depth. My pressure reading of the water outside the sub was currently at 5,200 bar, a bar being approximately equal to one atmosphere of pressure.

Each egg was lit. A very bright light, I might add. Hundreds of them covered the ocean bottom as far as the eye could see through the darkness of the vast ocean depths.

What are those things? I asked Cabal.

They are the Emissaries of the Watcher from the Sky, he responded.

Just then, I saw a nearby light go out, and the egg that had been there simply disappeared.

Where did it go? I asked.

Somewhere else in the galaxy, said Cabal. *To help the Watcher manage things.*

Manage what things? I asked.

Life, of course, he said. *The Watcher manages all life in the galaxy.*

But where do these eggs come from?

Cabal didn't respond with a thought. Instead, he raised his head slightly, peering out into the distance. I did the same, and soon I thought I saw movement. A few hundred meters away, something was moving above the vast bed of lighted eggs. Something large. And it was getting larger because it was approaching. When it was perhaps fifty meters away, it stopped. The lights from the eggs shone upon it but did not shine high enough to reach the top of the creature. All I could see was a dark, black mass that stretched perhaps three hundred meters across and rose up past the edge of the light, which penetrated the dark water around one hundred meters high. The creature was floating above the eggs. It had no appendages that I could see. It was simply a massive, dark shape floating in front of us. Suddenly, a circular light appeared on its body, about ten meters in diameter. The light was blinding, and I had to avert my eyes until I could command the clear shields over my eyes to adjust to it. When they did that, I glanced at Cabal as I brought my head back up and saw him staring directly into the light.

What is that creature? I asked.

The Mother of the Emissaries, he said.

I must admit, the sheer size of that thing frightened me to the core. Here we were, with this enormous creature, larger than any living thing I'd ever seen, and I hadn't even seen all of it yet. It hovered over its eggs, and I wondered if it was there to protect them from us.

Cabal, why are we here? I asked.

We are here to introduce you, he said.

Chapter 14

Do not fear, said Cabal. *You see, the Mother is not actually alive.*

What? How does it move?

I don't know, he answered. *But it doesn't matter. It does not go far, and it always stays within the radius of the mirage I spoke to you about earlier. It protects the eggs from the great creatures of the deep who might resent their presence.*

Cabal's comment about the colossal native life forms that lived down here intrigued me, but I needed to stay focused on this "thing" in front of me. *If it's not alive, how did it make these eggs?* I asked.

You have said it, he responded. *It makes them.*

So it's a factory?

Of a sort, yes. By the way, the eggs are very much exactly that. They are shells that protect what is inside.

What is inside, Cabal? I was nervous as to what his answer might be.

Intelligent beings, he said.

But why so many? And why so many different sizes?

Intelligent species from around the galaxy come in all shapes and sizes, he said.

Cabal explained that the massive structure in front of us had been placed there by the Watcher from the Sky, eons ago. As it turned out, Terrene was one of the best hiding places in the galaxy due to its tremendously deep oceans. And the presence of the Water People, whom the Watcher had converted to guardians of this secret place, was an additional safeguard. The Watcher decided which species needed her help and when, and that was when an Emissary was dispatched to their world to guide them on how to advance and continue on as a species.

Do you know if the Watcher has ever sent an Emissary to Earth? I asked.

I asked the Mother about this when Humans came to Terrene. The answer is yes. More than one. You seemed to recognize the shape of our city as if you had been there before. There is a similar city on Earth, is there not?

Similar, yes, I said, thinking about the Necropolis at Giza once again.

An Emissary brought that knowledge to Earth, he said.

What about Jesus, and Mohammed, and Buddha? Were they Emissaries from the Watcher?

I do not know, said Cabal. *I know nothing of Earth's history, only that the shape of our city was given to Earth by an Emissary from here.*

But why? I asked, so curious to know more.

I do not know, Charles, he said, seeming to grow impatient.

I'm sorry, I said. *I'm just bewildered at the moment. Why am I here again, Cabal?*

I have already told the Mother who you are and explained your powers. The Mother will now communicate with the Watcher, which might take some time.

What will we do while we wait? Should we eat?

It is difficult to make the eating arrangements at this depth, said Cabal. *The pressures are too tremendous to allow the opening and closing of the vents, which disburse the water and draw it back in. You certainly can understand that building a vessel that can survive at this depth is an outstanding achievement, and I must admit, the ship was created by the Mother on behalf of the Watcher.*

I understand, I said, wanting to know more. *I'll be fine without food. Can you answer more of my questions while we wait?*

I will do my best.

How long has all of this been going on? This factory at the bottom of the ocean?

That is not known, he said. *Indeed for many tens of thousands of years. Back so far that no one knows. The* knowledge and the right of passage to this place are passed down from one leader of the Water People to the next. Very few others know it even exists, and those who do are sworn to secrecy upon penalty of death. These pilots, for example, have sworn an oath of secrecy. They cannot even tell their own families.

That makes sense, I said. But what about the Land People? Why do they know nothing of this?

They have no need to know. An Emissary was sent to them by the Mother many tens of thousands of years ago, and that is when they were given the travel technology and the cloning technology. As far as they knew, the person who discovered these things was just one of them, not a gift from God, but a gifted person. Nothing more. And even that knowledge has long since passed from their history. They know nothing today of how their power to travel the skies and to live forever was obtained.

But you do, I said. And yet none of their tech was given to you.

We have our role to play, said Cabal. And we have never failed the Watcher, even when we cast out the Land People. After all, it was their destiny to go to space, or the Watcher would not have given them that technology. All we did was give them a firm push out of the door.

Interesting, I said. But upon their return, you decided to make a go for space yourself.

It is my prerogative as the leader of the Water People to make such decisions. The Watcher has given us no restriction in that regard. Just not much help. But then the Humans arrived, and things changed. For the better, I might add.

Thank you. And what of me, Cabal? What is it that you want of me?

It is not what I want. It is what the Watcher wants, if anything. And now we will know because the Mother has an answer for us. Please give me a moment.

During our entire discussion, Cabal's gaze never deviated from his focus on the intense round light on the monstrously large structure he had referred to as the Mother. His thoughts came to me and mine to him, but he never looked my way. It was as if he'd established some kind of communication link with the Mother that he dared not break. Some amount of time passed, I can't remember how much, but what I do remember is that every fiber of my being was telling me that this was the most crucial moment of my life, that if I genuinely wanted to become more, to become better, this was the moment when that would either happen or not happen. My heart beat in my chest, and my eyes, protected now by the blue-light protection I had initiated in my eye coverings, seemed to be locking onto the blazing yellow disk in the distance. Then my mind clicked, and a voice came into it. A voice that wasn't Cabal's.

Hello Charles, came the voice. *I am the Watcher from the Sky.* The voice was female and eerily familiar, although something was preventing me from attaching it to a physical body. *I speak to you through the Mother of our Emissaries, but it is my voice you are hearing, transmitted from far, far away from where you are now and in a different time. I am pleased to speak with you, Charles.*

From the moment the Watcher's first words came into my mind, I felt something I had experienced before. It was the feeling I had when I was communicating with OIM, that awareness in my brain that I was speaking to something bigger than myself. And that's when I knew that Cabal had been wrong when he told me the massive creature in front of me was not alive. But Cabal didn't know OIM like I do. That thing was made of OIM but did not come from me. It came from her, the Watcher. But I needed to keep this conversation going, so I tucked that tidbit of knowledge away for future use and spoke to her.

I am honored to speak with you, great Watcher from the Sky, I said, calm now because I was in the presence of something familiar. *How may I be of service to you?* I asked.

Will you come to me, Charles? We will speak about time and all that comes with it. Will you visit me, please?

Yes, but how? How do I find you?

Cabal will show you the way. I will see you soon.

The enormous round light went off, and the incredible voice was gone. I looked forward at the pilots and saw that they were slumped over in their seats, apparently dead or unconscious. I turned to Cabal, and his head was lowered into his hands. He was crying, and I reached over and touched him on his shoulder.

Are you alright, Cabal?

Slowly he raised his head and turned to me. *Yes, Charles, I am fine.*

Why were you crying then, if that is what it was?

Because I am the first of my kind to ever hear the voice of the Watcher from the Sky. She blessed me because of the gift I brought her.

What gift are you referring to? I asked.

I am referring to you, my friend.

Chapter 15

The pilots woke from their slumber, obviously not a party to the brief yet miraculous conversation which had just transpired. Cabal instructed them to return to the pyramids above. The journey took a little over one hour. We disembarked and swam up through the same passages as before, except we ended up in a different pyramid from the one where Cabal's throne sat on the top floor. I must have been mistaken on the path we took, but it didn't matter.

The lower two-thirds of this pyramid was the same beehive of activity as the other one, but everything changed when we swam through the hole to the upper floor. This was the pyramid with the darkened glass at the top. The glass prevented people from seeing in but somehow allowed the light from the sun to enter, so I had no trouble seeing what was in there, which was nothing, except for one of those eggs, like the ones we'd seen on the bottom of the ocean. This one was about two meters high and one meter in diameter at its wide point. It wasn't lit.

You will go inside this egg, said Cabal.

I'm thinking that's a no, Cabal, at least for now, was my initial response.

Cabal touched the egg, and it lit up, then a vertical line from top to bottom appeared and widened, creating an opening in the egg. On the inside was a comfortable-looking bench, placed inside the egg in a way that reminded me of one of those old photo booths from the twentieth century that I had seen during my travels. It was a half-moon shape, leaving space for a person's legs who was sitting there. But that person wouldn't be me unless I received some answers from Cabal.

Where is this egg supposed to take me? I asked.

To the Watcher from the Sky, of course, came Cabal's answer.

And how do I know that for sure?

Faith.

But I'm not a religious man, Cabal. I believe you know that.

I would go myself if I could, Charles, but I have yet to be invited.

Do you think she means me harm? I asked.

I think she means to make you more powerful than you are now.

How so? Any ideas?

I do not know Charles. But I can say this. If you do not go, I will kill you where you float.

Cabal's expression became predatory, and I remembered that he was part of a species that could be very aggressive when aggravated in certain ways. He'd seemed so civilized before, but now his sharp teeth and powerful arms looked terribly threatening. I forced myself to remain calm, thinking back to the moment, less than two hours previously, when I had spoken with the Watcher and what I had felt in my core at the time. And then it came back to me. This was it for me. If I was going to become more than what I was now, which was nothing more than a thief and murderer who'd gotten off on a technicality, this was the time for me to do it.

I swam up to Cabal and extended my arm to shake, and he grasped my hand and squeezed, his strength pouring through until I told the suit to resist.

Very well then, my friend, he said. *Until we meet again.*

I turned and swam to the egg, entered it, and sat on the comfortable bench. Cabal swam up to the egg and looked me in the eye.

Please ensure the Watcher knows that the Water People have kept the faith.

I think she knows that Cabal, but I'll be happy to tell her if you insist.

Tell her, please.

He touched the side of the egg, and it closed around me, sealing me in darkness, but somehow I felt pretty calm in there. I had no idea how much time passed, and I sensed no movement. I did not lose consciousness, nor did I struggle to breathe. People don't realize it, but water is nearly ninety percent oxygen by weight, the rest being hydrogen, so the contents of this vessel, while small, would last me for quite some time. I'd die of thirst before the oxygen in the egg ran out.

Nevertheless, I was nervous, and the more time that passed, the closer to sheer panic I came. There was no logical reason why. I'm not innately claustrophobic. If I were, I would have been gone from under the water some time ago, back to my comfortable home in New Madagascar, gathering with my wonderful friends at Murphy's pub for ale and good cheer. And as I reminisced about all I had given up, perhaps forever, depending on the outcome of this journey, the egg suddenly opened up. The water spilled from it onto the floor of a place I'd seen many times before. It was the time station in the Time Management building, back on Earth.

Chapter 16

I realized whose voice it was then, the voice of the Watcher from the Sky that had seemed so familiar. It was Annette's. But when she stepped in front of the egg to where I could see her, my confusion only multiplied.

"You'll want your suit to give you your legs back, Charles," she said, a pleasant smile on her beautiful face.

Stupefied, I gave the silent commands, and the suit rearranged itself, giving me the use of my legs. "I don't understand, Annette. Are you the Watcher from the Sky? How can that be so?"

As I approached her, she did something that baffled me. She rushed at me and embraced me with all her strength. She didn't cry out loud, but I felt tears from her eyes running down her face and onto my cheek since our faces were pressed together. I felt her trembling in my arms, but still, no sound from her. I resisted my own euphoria at being embraced by the love of my life after all these years and tried to determine the source of her emotional greeting. "Annette, what is it? What's wrong."

She pushed away from me and wiped away her tears. "It's just been a long time since I've touched another human being, Charles. Come with me, and I'll explain. Let's find a comfortable place to chat. You must have missed your wine down under the water. Am I right?"

She turned away before I could answer, and I followed her across the floor of the time station, dwarfed by the monolith that housed the Community of Minds, and I chased her as a new puppy would chase its mother. You have to realize that a mind like mine is rarely confused. On those infrequent occasions when it is, I become a very poorly functioning human being because all my concentration is dedicated to figuring out what is happening. Even walking was a chore, partially because I hadn't walked in well over a month but also because of my bewildered condition. Somehow, I managed to plod along behind her as she weaved her way to a pleasant room with a view of the city, offering me a seat in a comfortable chair, ordering wine from the coffee table, and handing me the glass. I sat and took a long pull, and it was magical, soothing my nerves and restless mind almost immediately. Annette sat, took a sip from her wine, and placed it on the table.

"Where do I begin?" she asked. "Perhaps I should first tell you when this is. It's 2749, nearly five hundred years in your future."

"So you've broken the law then?" I asked, still quite confused but at least a bit settled down from the glorious bouquet Annette had served me.

"There are no laws anymore, Charles," she said.

"What?"

"You need to understand something. I live here in 2749, and I am from this time. I didn't travel here from 2257."

"How?"

"I'm somewhat immortal now, Charles, like you. I used the cloning tech of the Land People in 2299 when I retired from the Department of Time Management. And then again in 2598 to renew myself. I've got another 150 years or so until I need another renewal, so hopefully, I'll have figured some things out well before then."

"What do you need to figure out, Annette?" I asked, perplexed.

"I need to determine why I'm the only biological human on Earth in 2749."

Flabbergasted, bewildered, and confused, all fall short of describing where my mind was at that moment. I was still waiting on an answer to my question regarding whether Annette was the Watcher from the Sky, but there were a lot of blanks to be filled in before that question became relevant.

"What happened?" I asked. "When did it happen?"

"I don't know what happened," she said, frustrated. "When I retired, I continued to live in my apartment here in the building, consulting with the new leadership on matters where my experience was relevant, but also enjoying life, traveling around the Earth and also to various planets we were at peace with. One morning in the year 2741, I woke up in my apartment and went to a meeting I'd been scheduled to attend. I saw no one along the way, and when I entered the meeting room, no one was there. One thing led to another, and it wasn't long before I concluded that I was the only biological human left on Earth. I used the controls in the time station to confirm that I was alone."

"You've been alone here for eight years, Annette?"

"Yes."

"And the Community of Minds?"

"They're here, thank goodness. Believe me, there have been days when I was tempted to go in there with them, but with no biological humans to monitor the status of the equipment, I thought that would be risky. But they've been an excellent resource for me. "

"So, what have you been doing for eight years?" I asked, wondering how I would survive without human contact for such a long time.

"Ah, now I can answer your first question," she said. "I've spent my time researching what went wrong."

"But my first question was, 'Are you the Watcher from the Sky?'"

"Yes, I am," she replied. "And that role is the basis of my research."

"Why didn't you go to Terrene for help?" I asked. "The time travel tech obviously still works. That's how you brought me here, right? But how did you do that without me having started my journey here in this time?"

"First, Charles, while all indications are that the time station here is completely functional, it doesn't work fully with me. I can send myself to the future, here on Earth, where I've found the same situation, i.e., no one home but me. And I can send myself back to when I was alone in 2741. But I can't go back any further than that, and I can't go to any other planets. I've tried dozens of times to send myself to Terrene and other friendly planets—and I don't go anywhere. But I can send inanimate objects out, and if I send the right kind of objects, communication can be facilitated, due to some improvements in the time travel tech made by the Minds, based on my request eight years ago. We can now observe what's going on in other times and places without going there, and if we can get someone to use one of the TT modules, we can bring them here. Like we did with you."

"You mean the eggs, right?" I asked.

"Yes, they do look like eggs. Their main function is to send the Emissaries to times and places on their home planets to seek help for Earth."

"Do you mean to find where everyone went and bring them back?"

"Yes, that's what I mean. But I've obviously come up short."

"Am I the first human you've brought here?"

"You're the first living thing I've brought here, Charles. I could have brought the clones from below the ocean, the hundreds of eggs you saw, but they know the whole situation and their missions due to the information transfer system we use with them."

"So why me?"

"I told Cabal to send you to me because while I hate to admit it, Charles, you are the best mind I know to help us get out of this mess."

"Don't you mean to help you get out of this mess?" I asked, regaining a bit of my swagger.

"Charles, if you are truly immortal, then you will be alive in this time. How would you feel if you found out that all human life on your home planet had been destroyed, or at the very least, removed?"

The irony of Annette's question wasn't lost on me. During my evil-doing days, I had plotted to destroy as much of humanity as possible using an OIM virus

I had created, and I would have succeeded if Dani and Annette hadn't reversed what I'd done using time travel. And now I was banned from Earth, my "home planet," and if my evil self still dominated my consciousness, I would rejoice at the news of humanity's demise on Earth. But I am happy to report that my primary reaction was fear and regret for all those who had been lost. But along with that, I realized that I wanted to help Annette, not only to save humanity but to help myself by trying to get her to see me as the new person I'd become. I needed to prove to her, once and for all, that I was good, that I had made myself back into the man she had once known. The guilt would always be there for me about what I'd done, but to be genuinely accepted by Annette, now and forever, would go a long way to assuage that guilt. And I told her as much.

"Annette, of course, I will help you. I would help you under any circumstances. But I need to understand a lot more of how you got from Point A in 2741, all alone on Earth, to Point B in 2749, still alone on Earth but somehow having made yourself into the Watcher from the Sky for the Water People in 2257. That's a tremendous leap that I can't imagine how you accomplished."

"I can do that," she said. "Let's have some food and talk further."

"No fancy restaurants to go to, I suppose?"

"The restaurants are there, and my guess is they'd even serve food if we went, but it's no longer completely safe to be outside here on Earth."

"Why?"

"I said the humans were gone," she said. "But the animals are doing just fine, expanding their horizons, actually. I've seen plenty of coyotes, a few wolves, and even a bear wandering around the city. It's safer to stay inside, especially since there are…other things out there."

"What kind of things, Annette?"

"Well, the weather has definitely changed, and it rains a lot more, and the wind sometimes blows extremely hard. And I think I've seen…"

She couldn't seem to get the words out, so I encouraged her. "What, Annette? It's okay. I'm here now."

"A ghost," she said, glancing down as if she knew I wouldn't believe her or think she'd gone mad, and I must admit that I was considering the latter, but I tried to lighten the mood.

"Wow!" I said. "It's a whole new world."

"So to speak," she said. "But not the kind of world I want to live in, alone."

"Tell me more about this ghost."

"After I see it, I'm unsure if I really saw it. It's like I see an image, and then I don't see an image."

"What does the image look like?"

"It's humanoid, meaning it has two legs, two arms, and a head, but it's all black. And it's massive, like a superhero villain or something. I call it a ghost because I'm not sure I've seen it all."

I had no reason to believe Annette wasn't being truthful with me, but it did cross my mind that perhaps she was becoming unhinged after so many years of being alone. Nevertheless, I tried to keep the conversation going without revealing my reservations. "How often have you seen the ghost, Annette?"

"Maybe a dozen times over eight years. Sometimes I'd wander the building, and when I was down in the lobby, I enjoyed looking out the windows at the streets. I'd often see the wildlife I mentioned. I once saw a pack of wolves and another time I saw a bear. But the lobby is also where I saw the ghost, looking in through the window, staring directly at me. But then, just as the image registered, it was gone. I've stopped going down to the lobby because I don't want to see it anymore."

"Have you ever seen it inside the building?" I asked.

"No, I haven't, thank goodness. That would really give me the creeps."

Annette was clearly shaken by this apparition, this ghost that might or might not be real. She was more vulnerable than I'd ever seen her, and I experienced a powerful urge to comfort her. I touched her on the shoulder, wanting to do more but afraid she might reject me. "It'll be okay, Annette," I said, my voice as soft as I could make it, then shifting to a more upbeat tone. "We'll figure it out. So let's get to it, then! Tell me what you're doing to make things right and how I can help."

Chapter 17

Annette explained how Earth had come to know so many alien species since my time frame. It all started after the battle with the Fury, the reptilian race that had tried to conquer Earth by enveloping it in a spherical white shroud, blocking nearly all the sunlight and causing the Earth to begin freezing. I was part of the team that had been dispatched from Terrene to fight them, and with the OIM freezers that I had concocted, based on tech initially developed by the Land People, we destroyed all life on the 108 alien ships that were surrounding Earth. Unbeknownst to us, word spread throughout the galaxy that the dreaded Fury had been defeated by a race of beings new to the galactic community of space-faring worlds. Humans from the planet Earth gained immediate respect throughout the galaxy. I found this somewhat frustrating since it had been humans and Land People from the planet Terrene that had saved Earth from the Fury, but such is the way myths are born, so I kept my mouth shut and listened as Annette continued her story.

Initially, out of fear, alien species from dozens of worlds reached out to Earth, offering to form alliances and peace treaties. Earth stalled for a while until they built the triple force field around the planet (also tech borrowed from the Land People) and reverse-engineered the offensive weaponry found on the captured vessels of the Fury. But after its defensive and offensive capabilities had been raised to the highest galactic standards, Earth reached out and began relations with many alien species. As the decades and centuries passed, technology was traded, except time travel technology, which Earth possessed but never used due to strict laws passed in my time, and once again, that was primarily because of me. The old me, I'll remind you, the one who didn't know right from wrong. The tech that was most valued by aliens was the cloning tech of the Land People because it provided a form of immortality most races coveted. And thus, by 2741, Earth had established strong relations with well over one thousand alien species.

The next part of Annette's history lesson (history that had yet to happen for me) was fascinating. This was the part about how she had made herself the Watcher from the Sky, using tech she'd had the Community of Minds develop, along with perhaps the most outrageous use of time travel dynamics I'd ever heard of. With the new tech from the Minds, she could now observe things as they were transpiring in different times using cameras that could transmit back to her along the time lanes carved out by the time station. And with the TT modules, the eggs I had seen at the bottom of the oceans of Terrene and used to come here, she could send physical objects to and from anywhere in the galaxy in any time frame. The enormous monolithic structure at the bottom of the Terrene Ocean was a TT module factory and a cloning facility. Annette had a database containing cloning specifications for literally every species Earth had relations with, and this was because one of the provisions of any trade of the cloning technology was permission for Earth to take a cloning scan of the alien species. In this way, Earth created leverage over these societies which encouraged them to remain peaceful since Earth possessed the potential to make clones of their kind, which could be used against them if needed. For example, Earth could create spies to infiltrate alien societies or build vast armies to fight civil wars on their home worlds. The result was that a level of peace had reigned throughout the galaxy that had never been seen before. Earth's philosophy of peace and harmony was now the predominant galactic ideology, even though it was backed up by the threat of force.

The first thing Annette had done was to grow a clone of the Land People and send it back thirty thousand years. This was her first "Emissary," but this one was of the clandestine sort. The clone simply became part of the ancient society of the Land People but eventually introduced the Land People to both the cloning technology and the travel technology. The Land People of that time believed this clone was simply an extraordinarily gifted person, and they had no reason to begin worshipping a deity since the technology was developed by one of their own.

The second Emissary was a Water Person, also sent back thirty thousand years. This one announced to the Water People that the Land People had been granted extraordinary gifts that would give them the power to live forever and explore space. The Water People were told that the grantor of these gifts was the Watcher from the Sky, the great goddess from above who watched over the galaxy and that if they followed her, she would build them a great city, and if they followed her rules, one day they would go onto the land and into space as well. The Emissary had OIM samples that would build the mountain upon which the great pyramids would be built and through which the tunnel to the bottom of the ocean would be bored. The deep water vessel was also made at that time from an OIM sample, and the Emissary drove it to the bottom of the ocean and deployed a sample to build the great factory, which would produce clones of all the alien species and the TT modules.

The Emissary to the Water People taught them the three Laws of the Sea and how to choose their leaders based on the ultimate goal of going onto the land and into space. I was amazed at how deftly Annette had used the chicken-egg phenomena that only time travel could create, giving tech we had acquired from the Land People, in my time, to the Land People thirty thousand years in the past, and teaching the Water People of thirty thousand years in the past about the laws of the sea and the Watcher from the Sky, using the information we had obtained from the Water People of my time about their heritage, passed down from generation to generation for thirty thousand years. Fascinating!

Annette's current focus was to use the Emissaries to seek help from each of their home worlds in explaining and correcting the inexplicable disappearance of all human life on Earth. But the answer was always the same. A species would contact Earth and receive a message back that all was fine. When ordered by Annette to go to Earth to verify these communications, the same findings were reported. All was fine on Earth in the year 2749. Everyone accounted for except Annette, who had inexplicably disappeared in 2741. Her hypothesis now was that she had been removed from humanity to inhabit another reality, as opposed to humanity being removed from her reality.

"So now I'm left with no choice but to send someone to 2741 to quietly determine if they can find out how and why I disappeared," she said.

"Who will be going back to 2741 Earth time?" I asked, already suspecting I knew the answer. Annette couldn't use time travel to go to the when she needed to reach, i.e., when she was still part of human reality, and a human would be much more appropriate for the secretive nature of this assignment than one of her Emissaries from other worlds. I suppose I could have simply read her mind to find the answer, but for some reason, I was reluctant to use this "little trick" on Annette. And it didn't matter because she confirmed the obvious then and there.

"As you've probably already guessed, Charles, that would be you."

Chapter 18

"Annette, I'm more than happy to go," I said, "but as I think about this, I sincerely believe we could use some more help."

"You're thinking of Dani and Aideen?"

"Absolutely. I know you trust them as much as you trust anyone, but it may interest you to know that I do as well. We've been through quite a lot together, on opposite sides and on the same side, but in either case, they bring out the best in me. Yes, I'm a genius; we all know that. But they make me more than that. They challenge me to think in ways I can't come up with on my own. They see things I don't see. If I'm going back to 2741 to find clues, I could use their help."

"And if I send you to them, you think you can convince them to come here?"

"I'm not sure," I said. "But I'd like to try."

Annette was quiet for a while, even longer than her usual pause, while she thought things through.

"What are you thinking, Annette?"

"I'm thinking I've called on them so many times already," she replied. "I just don't think it's fair to do it again."

"There's more at stake this time than ever," I countered. "And frankly, I think they're bored. Life on Terrene is peaceful, but those two like the action, and I believe they'd jump at the chance to help us."

"Well, when you put it that way," she said. "I'll program the time station to take you to them on Terrene."

"All right, let's go to the time station then," I said.

When we went to the control room, and Annette set the machine to take me to Terrene, at a time that was thirty-nine days after I'd departed to go under the sea, which is how much actual time had passed since I left New Madagascar for my underwater adventure. She gave me three time location devices—one for myself and one each for Dani and Aideen—and I went into the station and sat in one of the many seats. Before I left, a thought message from Annette came into my mind.

If Dani and Aideen decide not to come, please give them my regards from 2749. And come back soon, okay?

Yes, of course, I said. I'll be back straight away!

Annette's plea for me to return reminded me how terribly lonely she must have been, for eight years, all alone on planet Earth. I cautioned myself not to fall madly in love with her again simply because I had her all to myself. I was sure that her love for me would never be rekindled because of all the terrible things I had done, so I concentrated on the extraordinary galactic mystery that had led to all of this. Fascinating. Exciting! Another great project to keep me busy. *Thank you, Annette. I'll be back soon, hopefully with our two friends in tow.* And then, off I went.

I shook off the cobwebs after my entry onto Terrene. I was on the main street of town, outside of the administrative building where Clarion and Zephyr worked. Dani and Aideen might be in there, but they'd likely be elsewhere. I walked down the black streets, passing by the black buildings which composed the town, until I arrived at the white stucco structure with a gray slate roof that was Murphy's pub.

I entered the pub, seeing that it was relatively empty. Dani and Aideen were sitting at the bar with Orla. Liam was behind the bar, of course, but he didn't come out to put me in a bear hug as he usually did. He looked my way, and I could see that he was forcing a smile, and I knew something terrible must have happened. As I looked closer, I could see Dani, Aideen, and Orla quietly crying. Despite that, Aideen got up and came to greet me, embracing me and welcoming me back.

"We're happy you've returned from under the water, Charles, but this is a dark day for our little group here."

"What's wrong, Aideen?" I asked, my heart beating in anticipation of bad news.

"My clone back on Earth, and the younger Dani, decided to give up their bodies and join the Community of Minds."

"Oh my, I'm so sorry."

I walked over to the other two women and hugged each of them, expressing my condolences and wondering if I should try to find out more. Never one to shirk away from a sensitive subject, I plowed in.

"How did this happen?" I asked.

Dani was the first to answer. "They said they didn't fit in, that they felt they didn't belong there. They were always being compared to Aideen and me, and it made them feel unneeded."

"I'm sorry," I said. "But I thought people had to qualify through some rigorous standards to be accepted into the Community of Minds."

"They were granted admission based on 'Special Circumstances.' I mean, Danielle was from another reality, and Aideen was the first human clone made using alien technology, so it was easy for them to qualify."

"Did they tell anyone they were doing this?"

"Only Annette, who happens to be in charge of the Community of Minds as part of her responsibilities."

"And Annette told you, I assume?"

"She did," said Aideen. "And we weren't thrilled that she didn't consult with us first."

"I'm sure you gave her a piece of your mind, Aideen," I said, all the while thinking that the time to segue into my own mission might have arrived. "But Annette's got to respect the rules, and I'm sure client confidentiality is one of them. And she's got problems of her own anyway."

"How was your time under the water, Charles?" said Orla, seemingly uninterested in my comment about Annette, yet nevertheless trying to move the subject to another, less depressing topic than the biological end of Danielle and Aideen's clone.

"Amazing," I replied. "It was an adventure unlike any I've ever experienced, and I've had a few, mind you. I ended up in the year 2749 on Earth."

That got their attention. The three women's heads raised up, and they were staring right at me. Liam leaned across the bar and jumped in first.

"For fuck's sake, Charles, are you back to breaking the time travel laws again?" he asked.

"First of all, my old friend, the laws of Earth and the land on Terrene do not apply to the seas of Terrene. But it wasn't my choice to go there, anyway. It was someone else's."

"And who might that be?" he asked.
"The Watcher from the Sky."

Chapter 19

I explained the entire thing to everyone and waited for someone to react. Not surprisingly, Dani spoke first.

"Did Annette make the request for Aideen and me to come?" she asked, eyeing me carefully, probably to gauge whether or not I was telling the truth. But I had no reason to lie.

"No, that would be me," I said. "If I'm honest, I must say that she was somewhat reluctant to call on you two yet again. But I convinced her that we'd make very little progress with just me as the sole available time traveler since Annette can't travel."

"That's the real question, isn't it?" asked Aideen, "Why can't Annette travel?" She had a point and a good one.

"It's certainly relevant," I concurred. "But back to you two coming with me, if I have to grovel, I will. The truth is that I just don't think I can help Annette without your assistance."

"That's probably true," said Aideen, direct, as always. "Well, let's get on with it, then. You ready, my love?"

"Most definitely," said Dani. She raised her pint in the air. "Wish us luck in the future!"

Orla, Liam, and the rest of us hoisted our mugs and toasted, hugs were given all around, and we left the pub. Rather than head up the street to where the administrative building was located, we went the other way, to the less traveled part of town. We faced each other, counted to three together, then we all pushed our location devices. I arrived back in 2749 at the time station, in the building which had once been called the Time Management Complex but was known as the Space Exploration Center in that future time. After I got my bearings, I looked around for Dani and Aideen and didn't see them. I turned my head up to the control room and saw Annette through the glass, raising her arms up, palms to the sky, obviously wondering the same thing I was.

They said no? she asked, surprise in her tone.

Actually, they said yes. We all pushed the time location devices at the same time.

But they aren't here, she said. *What do you think that means?*

It means I need a glass of wine, and we need to talk.

Meet me in the lounge, she said. *You remember where it is, right?*

How could I forget? That place makes the best wine in town!

We met together in the lounge. I got some wine, but Annette declined, choosing coffee instead, as if she were preparing for a long strategy session. That was fine with me, but I thought I had it all figured out, so I expected our talk to be brief. As I sipped the delicious bouquet, Annette made it clear that we were on the same page.

"Time travel is one thing," she said. "Reality travel must be another kind of travel."

"Exactly," I said.

"Dani and Aideen couldn't travel here because they are living in Primary Reality, and I am not. And do you remember when the other Dani appeared, the one we called Danielle?"

This was a sore spot for me, although not a big one. "Yes, although I recall I wasn't consulted on the matter. You preferred the advice of Dani and Aideen on that one." I turned my chin up and pursed my lips, creating the look of pouting Charles, but it didn't slow Annette down, not one bit. She was rolling down the highway with her new revelation.

"Well, the funny thing is that we thought we couldn't bring her to us from the past because she was in a past that didn't exist, but it did exist; it was just a different reality. When she came to our reality, the Primary Reality, we could use time travel to move her to another time. But we couldn't bring her to Primary Reality from her alternate reality, just like we can't bring Dani and Aideen to our alternate reality from Primary Reality."

"But how was I able to travel here?" I asked, thinking I knew the answer already.

"The first time, it was the TT modules, the eggs as you call them. They were born from OIM samples made here, in this reality. Since they are from this reality, they can travel here and apparently carry whatever is inside them along with them."

"But how about this mission?" I asked. "I didn't use the egg to get here this time."

"I'm not sure," she said. "But maybe it's because you'd already been here. But it seems that if we want to, we can send some TT modules to 2257 on Terrene and bring Dani and Aideen here that way."

"Better off just sending a module with a message that we are dealing with another one of those separate reality situations and have things under control," I said.

"I'm fine with sending the message to them," she said, "but I hardly think we have things under control, Charles."

"We just have to gather more confirming evidence that our hypothesis is correct. I should be able to figure it out back in 2741?"

"Fine, but as I said, we certainly don't have things under control, Charles!" Annette appeared frustrated, but I was beginning to enjoy this puzzle. Perhaps my confidence would make Annette feel better.

"Yes, but we will. We don't need Dani and Aideen to help us figure this one out. I'll just go back to 2741 to determine what caused your reality to change, and then I'll come back, and we can figure out how to reverse it."

"Well, when you put it that way, it does seem like there's a ray of hope in my predicament."

"Absolutely," I said. "I'll leave first thing in the morning."

Chapter 20

Annette briefed me on the things I'd need to know to remain inconspicuous in 2741 and how things had changed from 2257. She informed me that technically, I was still banned from being on Earth, although I had been long forgotten in that time by everyone on Earth, except her and Aideen and Dani, who were also still alive in 2741. And please forgive me for saying this, but it was bloody upsetting to hear that after nearly five hundred years, I was still prohibited from coming to Earth, and it made me want to lash out at whoever was responsible for that. Unfortunately, I was very likely looking at one of the people who had prevented me from returning. On the other hand, five hundred years is a long time, and for all I knew, I had done something, or many things, which justified such a course of action against me. I would have to discuss this with Annette later, however, and therefore committed myself to the task at hand, allowing her to continue her briefing without interrupting.

Dani and Aideen had returned to Earth, full-time, soon after Aideen's clone and Danielle had gone into the Community of Minds, but they traveled a lot, especially to see Orla, Liam, Clarion, Zephyr, and Cabal on Terrene, all still alive and well in 2741. Dani's parents, Don and Pat Peterson, and all the others with Time Chain affiliations were also still around. But none of them came to the Space Exploration building anymore. When Annette saw them, it was usually at some function one of them had invited her to outside the building. This meant no one inside the building would question my presence there, especially if I was wearing a Space Exploration ID, which Annette would provide to me.

I asked her about myself in 2741. I wanted to know if I was still alive then, if my experiment to become immortal had continued to work, or in the worst case if I had used the cloning technology to renew myself every three hundred years, as everyone else had done. Annette was slow to respond, and I wasn't at all happy with what she told me.

"To be honest, Charles, no one knows if you were still alive in 2741 or not. You had seemed very happy on Terrene and initiated many projects over the years to improve the lives of Land People, humans, and Water People. You were well-loved there and seemed more content than I had ever known you to be. I visited Terrene after I retired, I think it was 2301, and you seemed great. You looked good, and you were full of energy. Fulfilled, I guess I would say."

"So what happened?"

"In short, you disappeared."

"When?"

"I don't remember, exactly, but it was hundreds of years after Terrene had been settled. There'd been some reports of you exhibiting erratic behavior, things like talking to people that weren't there and wandering the streets in the middle of the night. And then, you were gone. And we never heard from you again."

I was severely shaken by this revelation, so much so that the urge to abandon Annette's cause and take up my own entered my mind, but there would be time to deal with that problem after we rectified this one. I genuinely expected Annette's situation to be a quick fix. Then I could move on to tracking down my future self to see what kind of trouble I'd gotten myself into after hundreds of years of good behavior. I put my concern for my own well-being aside (which, by the way, made me immensely proud) and took up the cause to help Annette with clear eyes and a full heart.

"Okay, so no one will know me inside the building in 2741. But what if I have to go out of the building?"

"Why do you think you would have to do that?" she asked.

"I don't know, Annette, but if I'm going back to 2741 to find an answer, I think I should go where the clues lead me, don't you?"

"I suppose you should," she said. "And I appreciate it very much. But things are different on the outside, in 2741 compared to 2257."

"How so?"

"First, the Air-Rail method of travel has been replaced by the MRS. That's the Molecular Reconstruction System. You're familiar with the tech since it was given to us in your time by the Land People. Soon after that, Earth began replacing the Air-Rail terminals with MR terminals, and after a few years, we had a fully functional system. Now people can travel anywhere on Earth instantaneously, and there are stations to take them to the moon and Mars colonies as well. We still use ships for interstellar trips."

Annette explained how to use the travel system and then went on to describe the other life changes "on the outside," as she called it, and this made me wonder just how often Annette had left the Space Exploration building over the years. My guess was not much. She seemed to treat the outside as an almost undesirable place to be, and maybe for her, it was, after literally hundreds of years of living within the comforts of the building we were in at that very moment. She went on and on about this and that, and none of it seemed like such a big deal to me. The most interesting thing she said was that very few people worked anymore. AI and OIM did almost everything, and when combined with fusion power and solar power, the world would never run out of anything, and people lacked for nothing. Work was no longer necessary, so most people busied themselves doing things that interested them—art, science, writing, travel, and walking outside. There was still an entire staff in the Space Exploration building to deal with the hundreds of alien worlds and cultures throughout the galaxy, so I would encounter many people there. And on the streets, I would face even more. According to Annette, every day was a holiday on Earth in 2741, and the streets were packed nearly all day and night long.

After my briefing, Annette prepared my ID tag and implanted it into my forearm. The implant was programmed to give me full clearance to all business, recreational and residential areas of the Space Exploration complex. In short, I could go everywhere in the building. The final piece of business we debated was how long to set the failsafe for on the Time Station. The failsafe was the amount of time I would be allowed to be in another time before the station automatically pulled me back. And while I fully expected to return soon with the answers we needed, I reminded her that when I set out to do something, I would not be deterred by time. After all, we had all the time in the world to figure this out.

Nevertheless, Annette argued that I should report back to her periodically. I could tell she was anxious about being left alone again, so I suggested a compromise. Annette would equip me with one of the cameras that could transmit the goings on to her from other times. This way, I could speak with her and show her the things I was seeing, enabling us to set the failsafe for an extended period of time, and she could manually pull me back if I requested it or if she perceived I was in some kind of danger. We set the failsafe for one year, and she prepared the camera implant. This one was placed in the back of my neck, right where the spine meets the brain stem. It wasn't a camera, you see; it was a sensor that picked up and transmitted everything my eyes could see, and my ears could hear. A nifty little invention and I hardly felt it when she imbedded it in my spinal cord.

Annette and I embraced, and I could feel the need in her for human contact. I wondered if it could lead to other things if the situation stayed the way it was, just the two of us, alone together. I experienced a flicker of a daydream where we lived alone together in Annette's separate reality forever. Not a bad dream, but also not what either of us wanted in our lives. I didn't linger in these unrealistic musings for long, anyway, since we had a mission to complete. Getting back into the swing of the current assignment, I stepped away from her, went down into the time station, and she sent me back to 2741.

Chapter 21

I arrived in the time station itself, unused in 2741 except for the odd lecture or for gatherings with alien beings. I was on the station's floor, dwarfed by the ever-present monolith that housed the Community of Minds. I wondered if they could see me here. Did they have some alarm system that alerted them to an intruder in their external environment? I couldn't say, and it didn't really matter. I was here, and I had a job to do. The time of my arrival was six in the morning, not too early to be suspicious because people would be awake by then, some of them even working, and most importantly, it was before Annette had left her apartment the morning that she found herself in a different reality. It seemed logical that her apartment would be the first place for me to investigate.

I left the station and rode the invisible elevator to the 70th floor, a residential area for the highest-ranking Department of Space Exploration members. In

2741, Annette had long since been retired, but she was a person of particular significance on Earth, having overseen the first contact with an alien species, the first settlement of a planet outside our solar system, and the buildup of Earth's defense systems after the defeat of the Fury. The list went on and on, and it was no surprise that she was allowed to remain living in the residence she had occupied during her century of service in an official capacity. In 2741, she was still consulted regularly on various domestic and intergalactic matters and remained a prominent person, worthy of her address here on the 70th floor.

There were no guards on duty in the residential areas as they were an unnecessary intrusion on the residents' privacy and weren't needed because the AI took care of security here. My presence wouldn't set off any alarms due to the chip Annette had embedded in my forearm. I walked down the empty hallway toward Annette's apartment, wondering if I should go in. I knew from her briefing that she rose at 7 a.m. and was a heavy sleeper, so there was a good chance I could enter using the digital key to her apartment that was programmed into the implant. I didn't want to wake her up, at least not during my first trip here. If I could determine that waking her and removing her from the apartment before whatever happened, happened, I could do that on a return visit.

I telepathically told the door to allow me to enter, and the opening appeared in the solid black wall of the hallway. I slipped in, and it closed silently behind me. The apartment was still. Not a sound. I remembered from our time together, hundreds of years before, that Annette wasn't a perfectly quiet sleeper. She had a tiny, feminine snore that I found both relaxing and arousing. Sometimes, when I would wake up in the middle of the night and hear her pleasant sleeping noises, I wanted to possess her right then and there, but I was a polite lover, and it would be unproductive to make a habit of intruding on her sleep, uninvited. But there was no noise coming through the open doorway to her sleeping quarters.

I crept toward the bedroom, noticing how tastefully Annette had decorated her apartment. The art on the walls was especially intriguing. There was a framed photograph of the death mask of Tutankhamun, from around 1,500 B.C., certainly the most famous piece of art from Ancient Egypt and still one of the most admired pieces of art ever made. It was formed from two sheets of gold, hammered together, and precisely depicted the striped nemes headdress often worn by the pharaohs of old. As my eyes continued to survey the apartment's living area, I saw a replica of M.C. Escher's "Hand with Reflecting Sphere" from the 20th century. This self-portrait visualizes the artist's distorted reflection in the mirrored sphere. Painted in 1935, entirely by hand, it was a fantastic example of the power of the human mind to visualize abstract shapes. And there were many others, some from artists of more recent times that had not yet been born during my era. Annette's walls demonstrated her appreciation for the power of human creativity throughout the ages. This reflected her love for her profession, which had been time travel for most of her tenure.

As I came to the doorway and looked in, I saw that the bed was unmade but empty. Perhaps Annette had woken early and was in the bathroom, but the door to that room was also open, and no noise emerged. I tiptoed over to the bathroom and peered in. Nothing. Now I was becoming concerned. A quick inspection of the rest of the apartment validated my unease. Annette was gone.

I went to the living room and sat on the comfortable sofa to think, perplexed and confused about what to do next. I suspected I would need to come back even earlier until I could pinpoint the exact moment she disappeared. And then, I could simply wake her and tell her we needed to get out of the apartment and go to another part of the building, preventing whatever took her from doing it. I decided to go back to Annette in 2749 and talk this through. I reached for the time location device but suddenly experienced a brief moment of wooziness, my mind nearly blanking out. It felt like a time jump. When I regained my senses, I looked up, and standing in front of me was a massive being with two legs, two arms, and a bald head, but the color of its skin, even its face, and head, was as black as obsidian. However, its eyes looked like an average human's; I believe the color was hazel. It was more than a head taller than me, had a large chest and a thin waist, with bulging biceps and thighs. I was dreadfully concerned that this creature meant to harm me, but then a thought entered my mind.

I am the one who moved Annette, Charles. And now, I will take you on a journey of your own.

Chapter 22

The monster in front of me, which was very likely the apparition Annette had called the "ghost," suddenly disappeared. I was shaken, not only because now I knew who was responsible for the foul play that had banished Annette to a reality void of all human life except herself, but also because I was frightened. The thing had loomed over me in a threatening way, and it was so large and powerful that I'm sure it could have crushed my skull with one of its gargantuan hands. But I had no time to catch my breath because, in the next instant, I blacked out, losing all sense of self and awareness of my surroundings.

*****

I came to my senses beside the old car park on the mainland side of the channel, across from Omey Island.

I found myself in a cold, driving rain and wondered when I was. It certainly wasn't 2741 because I knew the car park had been covered over long ago since there were no longer any cars in future times, and also because there was an actual automobile in the lot. You will remember that I remain the most prodigious time traveler of all time, and I know my history better than most, and while I couldn't name the model and make of the vehicle, I knew it belonged to Aideen. I'd seen it parked many times in her driveway at her cottage on Omey Island. My guess that this was 2022 was confirmed when I saw Dani run into my line of vision, approaching the vehicle. The driver's side window was down a few inches, and I heard Aideen's voice, muffled by the wind and rain but unmistakable. Dani ran around to the passenger's side of the car and got in.

I stood there in the rain, the ghostly sound of its impact with land and water making a hissing sound all around me, the wind howling from time to time as it gusted, and I wondered what it was that I was witnessing. Was this the moment when they had met for the first time? Probably. And then it hit me. I did that. Without me and my admittedly heinous intentions in using the Time Chain to find a way to destroy the future, these two would have never met. A wave of ebullience washed over me, dousing any regret for my malicious intent during that horrible time in my life and instead reminding me that not all of the fallout of my actions had been bad. These two had become two of the most accomplished and honored citizens of the 2250s, and their love for each other was pure and enduring. There was no denying that I was responsible for it. At the very least, one could say I planted the seed that allowed their love and heroics to bloom.

The rain had stopped, and I noticed the car pulling out of the lot and easing down into the causeway, now emptied of water by the outgoing tide. The vehicle drove out onto the sand and sped across, receding into the distance, but I could see it reach Omey Island and turn left, making its way to Aideen's quaint little cottage. But my euphoria was also receding, and I wondered what to do next. I thought about where I might go in 2022. Indeed, I had been here many, many times, visiting the great cities of the world, as well as Aideen and Dani in the cottage across the channel. But as I searched my mind and heart for direction, the answer was suddenly obvious.

I stepped out of the car park and turned toward the causeway, walked down the ramp, and began to follow the signs on poles across. When I reached the center of the channel, I turned left, knowing precisely where I was headed. I remembered that after a few hundred meters, I'd see a large rock just to the right of me. And sure enough, there it was. I went over to the rock, took ten paces back toward the mainland, knelt down, and dug in the sand. Soon I uncovered the hatch, opened it, and entered the first chamber. I placed my hand on the far wall, and the opening appeared. My old friend still recognized me! I followed the tunnel down and came to the next wall, placed my hand on it, and entered through the opening that appeared into the heart of the time station. The chamber was lit from above, and I could see the two time cradles and the circular launch platform nestled in between them. A feeling of warmth enveloped me, the sense you have when you come home after a long absence.

I sat down on one of the cradles and squeezed its edges with both of my hands, feeling the warmth of the black stone, the living substance that I was more of an expert in than any other biological human. And as I thought of it, I suspected I had come to know more about OIM than even the Community of Minds, its inventors. I had gone further than the Minds because I had performed experiments on myself they could not conduct themselves because I had a body, and I could introduce OIM potions of special significance into my organism, elixirs that would give me powers that even the Minds did not possess. Immortality was just one of the many gifts my experiments had provided. I could also communicate telepathically, read minds to some degree, and command the OIM to do my bidding, something the Minds could not do, to the best of my knowledge.

As I reminisced about my greatness, I stood and wandered over to the launch pad, where the travelers would be transported while holding the hand of the time link. I stepped onto the circular platform, wondering if I now had the power to send myself to another time without using a time link simply by telling the OIM of this station to send me there. But before I had time to test my theory, a wave of dizziness overcame me, and I blacked out once again.

Chapter 23

I appeared just outside a scruffy little cottage I remembered well. The year was 1801, and the town was Claddaghduff, directly across the channel from Omey Island. It was the home of sixteen-year-old Ciara, and as I peered in through the foggy window, I first saw the dead woman lying face down on the floor, over near the hearth. It was Ciara's mother, killed by her father in a fit of carnal rage. I turned my head to the left and located the father on the bed, trousers down around his ankles, raping poor Ciara with abandon. The dark-haired girl screamed in agony from the physical pain but even more from the emotional pain. Her father was doing this to her, and the scars from that barbarian act would be with her for her entire life. Ciara was now a grown woman, living in 2257, as the rest of us were, but I had to believe that when she had nightmares, this horrible experience got top billing.

Next, I witnessed the time travel arrival of myself and Dani, still holding onto the girl's hand and wrist. I was facedown against the wall, and Dani was face up, on the other side of the bed, with Ciara and the red-haired rapist between us. I yanked my hand free from the girl's wrist, got up on my knees, and extracted the Tickler, killing the man on the spot. When I pushed him off the bed, Dani fell off with him, but she rose quickly, and well, you know the rest.

Dani chastised me for killing the man, among other things, and as I stood outside the cottage and reluctantly watched things unfold inside, I knew in my heart that I didn't have to kill that man. The harsh reality is that I had wanted to kill him. I could have easily set the Tickler to stun, which would have served our purposes equally well because I could have knocked him out for half an hour, and we would be gone when he woke. But that's not what I did. I killed him. And I enjoyed doing it.

It had been a long time since I had killed a human. The last two had also been in 1801, during my visit after escaping from 2253 by the skin of my teeth, befriending old Liam Murphy, and then killing the men they'd sent to hunt me, dumping them into the OIM that was building my new time station, letting it eat them up as it did everything else it touched. I was completely gone at that point, enveloped in the hazy fog of a heroin addict, only I was an OIM addict, seeking immortality and regretting nothing, no action, no matter how malevolent it was. At the time I killed Ciara's father, I wasn't quite as far gone, but the one difference in that killing from all the others was that I had wanted to do it. One evil man saw another committing an immoral act and killed him. I remember thinking I was actually doing good at the time, ridding the world of one piece of vermin it could do without. But no, that wasn't the truth of it. I relished the act of killing that man at my core.

I wandered away from the cottage, people on the streets offering bewildered stares at the man dressed in a skintight yellow suit that was actually my own skin, stumbling down the muddy streets as a drunk would plow home from a night at the pub. It didn't take me long to figure out where I was going, and I glanced back to make sure no one had followed me. Apparently, I was as frightening as an alien from another planet because the coast was clear. I made my way to the time station and went into it, ending up sitting on the launch pad again. My feet were planted firmly on the floor, and my arms were wrapped around my knees. I rocked back and forth, back and forth, trying to rid myself of the evil that lived inside me.

The comfort of the time station, which I had made with my own hands and mind, helped me regain my composure. This was my sanctuary. I had lived more years inside this vessel of black stone than anywhere else, and even though at times I had wanted to pull my hair out from claustrophobia, boredom, or the simple need for the companionship of someone I loved, someone, anyone, to take me away from the path I had chosen, I still loved this place. I was safe here until Dani and Annette schemed and took it from me.

It had taken me years to rid myself of my hatred for them both, even though I knew I loved Annette and respected Dani as much as any human being I had ever met. But I had succeeded. I had freed myself from hatred, committed myself to do good, and I had done many good things and no evil stuff for quite a while now. Unfortunately, this return trip to witness the rape of poor Ciara, and my unrepentant murder of her father, had provided a vivid reminder that I had evil in me. The potential to do evil. Was it the OIM addiction, or was it just who I was? I didn't know the answer, and I was given no more time to contemplate this critical question because, once again, my consciousness was taken from me.

Chapter 24

Now I was somehow looking down on my prison cell in the Time Management building, in the year 2254, I presumed, hovering like a ghost above the meeting I had with Dani and Aideen, the one when I revealed my plan to stop the Land People from destroying all human life on Earth. None of them could see me. I wondered if I were somehow invisible, and for a moment, I reflected on all the things I had yet to learn about how the universe works. At the time, I wasn't at all certain that I wasn't already dead, and perhaps I was a real ghost, acting the way spirits do, you know, hovering and spying on the life they no longer shared with those they loved. All of that rot now seemed so real, so true. There was my living self down below, and neither I, Dani, nor Aideen could see or hear Charles, the ghost, hovering just above them. But I could see and listen to them.

"It doesn't matter," said Aideen. "Tell us what you need to tell, and we'll be on our way. Seems you've got yourself in the middle of yet another crisis, Charles. Now, how do you propose to save the world?"

Ah, yes, that comment from Aideen just about summed it up. I was going to save the world. And I did, although it turned out to be a false alarm since the Land People were bluffing. But it was my intention to help, you see, and even though I had offered my assistance in exchange for my freedom, the point seems to be that here was a turning point in my life. Here was a lesson I had learned that I could, in fact, do good things if I put my powerful mind and my duplicitous heart into it. Suddenly, everything went black.

*****

My next destination was space, above the planet of Terrene, hovering again. This time I was up near the ceiling of Return One, the first ship sent to Terrene to reclaim the land using the plan I had developed. And I was basically in charge of that mission; Clarion was the official commander, but she did very little on that first voyage. It was me running the show, and I built the entire island, the one known as Base One, a boring name and not nearly as appropriate as my name for the place, New Madagascar, because it was almost exactly the same size as the island country of Madagascar on

Earth, and had a similar shape. But I digress. The point of this visit was obviously to show me my continued development in the name of good. After all, I settled a new world on behalf of its original inhabitants and the settlers from Earth. Never done before. All that. And the people who went there, both Land People and humans, were the happiest you'll find anywhere in the galaxy, I'll wager. Blink.

*****

I remained in space, hovering this time inside one of the nine vessels sent from Terrene to do battle with the Fury. I had invented, well, I had engineered an OIM freezer based on an old design of the Land People, supervised the deployment of such freezers inside 108 enemy vessels, and killed every living thing on board that fleet of aliens who had attacked Earth and attempted to make it their own. And let me be clear, this was not murder. This was war, a war we had not started, mind you, and I returned home to Terrene, a war hero. I was really tasting the sweet nectar of good at that point and wanted to do more. Blink.

*****

And now I was on Diaspora Ten, confronting the rogue Land People who had powerful weapons on their ship and were threatening human life on Terrene, all life actually if the humans did not comply with their demands and leave the planet. I had developed the ability to perform minor miracles by then, and I projected that hologram of the good times on Terrene, and then I produced the OIM sample that could destroy the entire ship, and then the Land People of Diaspora Ten submitted to my will and surrendered. I returned home, once again a hero. Blink.

*****

Next, I was out in the backyard of my wonderful cottage on Terrene, building the time station that would enable Aideen's clone to be made, three years younger than the first Aideen and precisely to the specifications Dani and Aideen had wanted. Why did I do it? Because those two were my friends. My best friends, if I'm honest, along with Liam. And what good is a friend if you can't do something good for them, something they want and need very badly. So I did it, at risk to my own well-being and good standing on Terrene, hard-earned, I'll tell you, and Annette did come and destroy my little station, but that was the extent of my punishment. But it didn't matter. I was going to help my friends, no matter what. And I'm sure that was the lesson here. Despite all the evil things I had done in my life, I had turned my life around through sheer force of will. I had become good. And this was what it was all about. This was the lesson the black beast was trying to teach me. That I was good. Unfortunately, my next destinations proved this initial conclusion to be categorically wrong.

Chapter 25

I regained consciousness standing on the top of a tall mountain, surrounded by what seemed like an endless mountain wilderness. The sky was blue, and there were very few clouds, although the wind was brisk. Based on the weather, I assumed it was late spring, but I had no idea what year it was. I looked south and saw Mount Snowden, Wales's tallest mountain. To the north was Ben Nevis, the tallest mountain in Scotland and in all of the British Isles. To the West was the Irish Sea, and I could clearly see the Isle of Man sitting there on the left side of my view, and a little further, to the right, was the Ards Peninsula of Northern Ireland. These were sights I had seen before, and I knew I was standing on top of Scafell Pike, the tallest mountain in England, which was around twenty kilometers, as the crow flies, from my childhood home in Ambleside. I wasn't cold because the skinsuits were impervious to cold and wind, but I wondered if he was going to make me walk all the way to Ambleside, which would take five or six hours. As I circled around, enjoying the view, I caught sight of a boy sitting on a boulder on the eastern side of the summit. The boy's mouth was stuffed full with a sandwich he'd been munching, but he'd stopped chewing, his eyes wide in amazement, as if he'd seen a ghost. A smile came to my face because after seeing the boy, I knew what year it was: 2158. And the boy was my nine-year-old self, off on a day of mischief and adventure when I should have been doing my lessons. I felt I was getting closer to the conclusion of this time travel kaleidoscope, and right on schedule, the world flashed out, once again.

*****

I woke, standing on the street outside of my childhood home. I followed the walk in the front yard, ambled up the steps to the front porch, and peered into the window to the left of the door. The house seemed unlived in. I tried the knob, and the door opened. I entered.

The house was obviously in the process of being emptied and readied for sale, so this must have been 2161, not long after my parents succumbed to the plague that swept the world that year, one of many such plaques that weren't stopped until the immunity pills were invented by the Community of Minds. I had been shipped off to boarding school, and William, my older brother, had undoubtedly been dispatched for his first year at University. The money from the sale of the home and its belongings had been needed to help pay for both of us to be where we'd been sent, to continue on with our lives without Mum and Dad.

The living room was directly to the right of the entrance, and I saw him sitting in my father's favorite reading chair. He beckoned me to enter, waving one of his massive black arms toward the tweed sofa my mother had loved so much. On their days off and in the evenings, the two of them would sit together, reading and enjoying tea together; not a word of conversation between them, but it gave me comfort to know that they were sharing time and space together. But now here was the hideous beast I'd first met in Annette's apartment, occupying Dad's favorite chair, barely fitting in it, his massive hips nearly touching the armrests, whereas for a normal-sized man like my father, a gap of several inches would be present on both sides.

I assumed I had no choice but to follow his commands. After all, he'd been whisking me around through time and space without my consent for the past several hours. I had no sense of how long I'd been following this modern-day Ebenezer Scrooge adventure, viewing my acts of both good and evil during my life. I also had yet to learn why he'd done it. By the way, I refer to him as "he" because he did indeed have the physique of a male, although he was quite a bit more massive than a normal human being. Anyway, I stepped over to the sofa and sat, waiting for whatever came next.

You must have questions, said his voice inside my head.

I don't know why, but perhaps because of my presence in my childhood home, I didn't want to send thoughts back to him. Most of you know that I'm not an innately courageous person, although you have seen that I can summon the courage to do what must be done when confronted with difficult circumstances. I most definitely can feel fear, but I can overcome it through the force of my will when necessary. In this case, however, I wasn't afraid. More to the point, I was actually terribly angry with the black monster because he was the one who had banished Annette to another reality, which contained no intelligent biological beings except herself.

As if reading my mind, which he undoubtedly was, the beast responded to my line of thinking and also addressed my outrage.

Yes, Charles, I told you it was me. But you would want to know the why of it, wouldn't you? Perhaps that will soothe the simmering rage I feel within you.

I took a moment to ask myself why his telepathic voice seemed so unemotional, so generic, as would the voice of an AI-generated voice. I wondered if he was some kind of AI humanoid, or if he was disguising his real voice for some reason yet to be revealed. "The why of it would certainly be a good place to start," I responded, knowing that I wanted much more than that from this creature in the end.

Very well. And since you seem to prefer the spoken voice, "henceforth, I will address you in that way."

The shock of hearing the monster's spoken voice was beyond anything I'd ever experienced. The agony it culled up inside me, beyond words. The fear. The knowledge. The why of the things that had happened. Because it was my voice. The beast was me.

Chapter 26

"I am you, many hundreds of years later," said my voice.

"What are you?" I asked, already putting the pieces together but wanting him to confirm my suspicions.

"I have evolved into a more advanced form of the OIM-human hybrid than you are, currently."

So it was true. The trend was already there. My telepathy, my mind reading, my ability to produce OIM samples of virtually any variety in the palm of my hand, and my ability to communicate with the OIM consciousness. These were the physical manifestations of my early evolvement into the OIM Monster who now sat in front of me. A closer inspection of the skin showed it was a coating of pure OIM, black as the darkest ocean depths, smooth as a baby's skin, but undoubtedly impervious to almost any form of physical force. I wondered how deeply the OIM had progressed into my body. Were my muscles, my bones, my organs made of OIM? My brain? I dared not ask the monster such questions because I was afraid of what his answers might be.

And even though the skin was black, the eyes were mine. I wondered how they had remained unchanged from what they were now, brown hazel, sometimes changing when the light was just right to more of a green hazel, but they seemed to be my eyes. The eyelashes were still there as well, medium length and dark, like the hair on my head, which was gone from the beast's gigantic skull, now a spherical orb of non-reflective black. It was a lot to take in, but the worst was that this hideous creature in front of me was the absolute manifestation of where my future would take me. It wasn't a pleasant feeling. But of course, there was the why of it, as he'd mentioned. Why were we here? Why had he punished Annette in this way? And since he could read my mind, he jumped in and gave me the answers.

"Annette has already told you that somewhere down the line, you disappeared. Slipped away from the known world, never to be seen again. Of course, that was deliberate. You've not yet experienced the flashes, the brief transformations to this, then the flash back to human. But it will come, and you won't be able to control it. Fearing embarrassment and humiliation, you will recede into the background, using your newfound powers to travel through time and space without the need of a time station or any other physical assistance."

"How did you get so big?" I asked. After all, he was a head taller than me and much more broad and muscular.

"Frankly, I can make myself into any shape I want to," he said. "I decided that if I was going to be an ugly OIM monster, I might as well mold my body into something magnificent. Small consolation, really, but it gives me some comfort to look like Hercules. But there's much more, involving Annette and alternate realities that I need to explain to you. You need to understand how we arrived at this moment."

He told me the first thing he did after deciding to leave the civilized world was to travel back to Earth, to one of the unoccupied barrier islands off the Irish coast adjacent to Omey Island. He was simply looking for a place to think, undisturbed by humans, and he knew this was a spot that people rarely approached, and when they did, they didn't stay long. There was nothing there.

"I needed to be alone, and I needed to process one thing that was a thorn in my heart, driven further into my gut, time and time again, by the one person I loved more than any other. Of course, you realize that would be Annette."

"I know some of that story," I said. As you know, Annette had been my assistant back in the day and had turned me in for my plan to abscond with the time station technology. Next, she spent seventy years trying to catch me, rising up in the ranks of EarthGov politics on the back of what I had given her. And eventually, she succeeded. But after she finally caught me, I found a way to negotiate my release and lived my life on Terrene, relatively untouched by Annette's power back on Earth. I'd come to grips with all of this, but there must have been something more, and I asked as much of this demon that was a future me. "Was there something else? Did she do something else that upset you?"

"Of course she did," he said. "After all the good I had done, for Terrene, for Earth, for the galaxy in general, she continued to block my every effort to be allowed to return to Earth. I didn't even want to live there. I just wanted to visit and enjoy the life available on a planet basking in the glow of technological and environmental balance. But she wouldn't allow it. Even after she retired, she would never fail to use her influence to have my visa applications for Earth rejected. And with no good reason."

Annette had mentioned that I was still banned from Earth, and while I suspected she was part of the reason, we hadn't really discussed it. My feelings on the subject had been mixed, but I was by no means ready and willing to do to her what this monster had done. "So you decided to banish her to some alternate reality with no intelligent living beings? Was not being able to come to Earth so important that you would take a person's life from them and ruin it?"

He sat back in his chair and seemed to be reflecting on whether or not to reveal something, but then he did. "It's the opposite of that," he said. "I wanted to put Annette in a place where only one other living being could be with her. A person who loved her more than any other. A person that was still more human than OIM in 2257."

"And, of course, you are speaking of me," I said, and then I disappeared.

*****

I regained my senses while walking along an avenue in what I knew to be Brussels. The streets and buildings were black, so I knew it was after OIM had been invented and literally taken over the world. But the streets were empty, save for a lone couple around ten meters in front of me. They were holding hands, taking a leisurely stroll, both with long dark hair, his tied back in a ponytail and hers flowing gloriously like a silky main down her back. Of course, it was Annette, and me. I stopped in my tracks when a wolf appeared from an alleyway and dashed toward the couple, who had also stopped. The man raised his hand, beckoning the wolf to come to them, and it did, lowering its head to be pet. The couple continued, and the wolf trotted beside them, soon joined by several others.

I'm not sure I've mentioned it before to you, but when I lived under the water, I learned from the Water People how to communicate with many of the other species that shared the sea with them. It came very naturally to me, especially since I no longer needed a handy to facilitate telepathy. As you will remember, thinking is simply synapses and neurons coalescing in a certain way, having nothing to do with language. It was, therefore, a simple matter to communicate with the life under the seas of Terrene. And I could obviously do it with wolves, too, as demonstrated by the man I was following. Me. Alas, my voyeurism was temporarily interrupted by a time jump.

*****

I appeared on the same street several years later, apparently, because now two small children were walking along with the couple, one holding the mother's hand and the other holding the man's. The wolves were still following along as if they were part of the family. Seeing this, of course, was a painfully emotional moment for me. My most heartfelt dreams. Real. And soon, I would hear the rest of the story. Blink.

Chapter 27

I was back in the living room of my childhood home in Ambleside, sitting on my dead parents' tweed sofa, facing my future self, who remained in my father's favorite chair, and while I hated him for being there, I appreciated the fact that now he was going to tell me, specifically, just what kind of trouble I was in, this time. But before I tell you what he told me, I want to disclose a thought I'd been having ever since the monster revealed that he was me in the future. The issue I'd been wrestling with was what to call him. The idea of calling him "Charles" was nauseating. A non-starter. I just couldn't accept that I would become this thing, that I had to end up as a hideous, albeit powerful, outcast from society. I had worked so hard to immerse myself in my community on Terrene, with some success, and it hurt too much to know that it wouldn't last.

I decided to find a way to turn my future in a different direction. I didn't know how, but I would do it.

Therefore, this thing in front of me wasn't me, and I would give it a name that meant something altogether different. It didn't have to be a repulsive name, like the "Hideous Beast" or the "OIM Monster," in fact, I wanted it to be something that gave me hope yet clearly identified him as something different. So I settled on "the Anomaly." I wouldn't call him that to his face, but I would explain my logic to Annette later, and I will use that name henceforth in my narrative. Anyway, back to the Anomaly's explanation of what, exactly, was going on.

Here is what he had to say: "During the visits to your past that I've just sent you on, Charles, you have witnessed many of your acts of evil, and you have observed your recent run of good deeds on behalf of humanity. And in your visits to the future, the future you and Annette will have, you wonder how long that will last. Because as you sit here, gazing at me in horror and apprehension, hoping beyond hope that the things I tell you are lies and that the hideous being in front of you is not truly yourself, not truly your future, you know in the deepest recesses of your gut that I am your future, Charles. That I am, indeed, you.

"I can take you through it, step by step, our horrible transition into what we are now, and it's not a pleasant story. Imagine the first time I looked in the mirror and saw myself reflected as OIM Man, only for an instant that first time, and then I flashed back to being you again, still more human than OIM. It wasn't like a patch of black appeared on my skin somewhere, an arm, a leg, my torso, my face, and then slowly spread, taking over my body one agonizing step at a time. No, it was a flash to this and then a flash back to that. At first, it only happened every week or so, and usually when I had just woken up in the morning. I would go to wash my face at the sink, brush my teeth, and then I would look up and see a monster staring back at me in the mirror. This OIM Man still had my long dark hair—it was only later that I decided to make the hair go away—but he had the obsidian skin you see now, and as time went by, the flashes became brief visits, and then he would visit daily, and would stay for breakfast, and then for lunch, etc., etc.

"At that point, I couldn't go out anymore, and I secluded myself in the cottage above the cliffs of New Madagascar, and it was lucky that by that time, Aideen and Dani had moved back to Earth because when they were on Terrene, they came to visit me regularly, and I couldn't have them or anyone else seeing me like this. So I planned to leave, and I needed to figure out where or when to go. By then, the OIM had informed me that I no longer needed a time station to travel, that I was a time station. But there was more. The OIM told me that, on its own, it had cracked the code for traveling between realities; therefore, I was also privy to that ability.

"You may remember the theory of separate realities espoused by the Community of Minds during your times, that time travel was the sole cause of alternate realities and needed to be banned to avoid creating more of them because these realities would encroach on the Primary Reality and cause all sorts of problems, none of which had ever been proven. But here's the truth. There is no Primary Reality. There are an infinite number of realities, and the ones created by time travel are just a grain of sand on a beach in the contest of creating realities. Realities create themselves, and there is no limit to how many of them there are; they do not encroach on one another.

"Time travel cannot cross from one reality to another. That is why Annette is stuck where she is. It's a different reality, chosen for her by me since I can cross from one reality to another as easily as opening a door and walking into another room. And no one from your reality can go there to her, except me slash you. It's not the TT modules, the eggs, that Annette developed. It's because you are me, Charles, that you can go to her while no one else can. You've had the ability to time travel and cross between realities for some time already without assistance from machines.

"And so now we come to why you are here, and it might surprise you. You see, I need your help in making a decision, Charles. You are in the very early phases of becoming what I am, and I must tell you that after hundreds of years of being what you will become, I can't remember what it's like to be a normal human anymore. Perhaps you can't either, but my guess is that you will have a better appreciation than I do of why being human is worth it because we have the opportunity to become that again if we decide that is what we want. At this point in your life, Charles, you've clearly figured out that while you have the potential to do evil things, you also have the potential to do good things. And your recent string of good behavior is a vital sign that you know what you want. I brought you here, Charles, to show you that you can't have the life you want to live because all roads lead to me, with one exception.

"I wish I could say thank you," I said, "but that's not terribly good news."

"I understand, but there is also hope. There are choices you can make that will take your life down a different path."

"How so?"

"Your life can take three paths, Charles. Path One is the way you've been traveling until now, and it leads to me. Path Two leads to a life with Annette, alone in a reality with no intelligent beings other than you two, but it won't last because, eventually, you will become me. Path Three leads back in time to the moment you decided to steal the time travel tech that led to the construction of the Time Chain. Suppose you make a different choice at that moment. In that case, you and Annette can stay together in a more normal reality, a world shared by all humanity, and enjoy a life together doing good things, and all of the evil things you've done would be in a different reality. This reality, actually."

I thought about what he was saying, offering, really. It was a sad state of affairs for me, but it was what it was, and I had to face it. There were pluses and minuses to each option. Path One meant that I would eventually become the beast sitting in front of me, and I would be an outcast from human society and probably from most other societies as well. Yet I would be the most powerful being in the galaxy, able to move through time, space, and realities with ease. Nevertheless, being an outcast was a lot to take. Too much, and it wasn't clear to me why this had to be so, anyway.

"How certain are you that my friends, like Dani, Aideen, Liam, Orla, and most importantly, Annette, would reject me simply because I have a different appearance? "

"It's more than a different appearance, Charles!"

"What?"

"I am an evil being!" he shouted. "I want to do bad things. Do you realize I created the reality I sent Annette to? I disposed of all intelligent living beings on Earth and enjoyed every minute of it. Snuffing out the lives of billions. And the cherry on top of the ice cream was placing Annette in the reality I had created, just for her, punishing her for all she's done to us. I loved it! I'm still basking in the glory of it all. But now I have you to talk some sense to me, the Charles who still wants to do good. Talk to me, Charles. Tell me to go with you, back to that moment, to the moment you decided to break the law to steal the time travel tech. Tell me to help you convince our foolish self to take the more noble path. Then both you and I will never exist, but the Charles you want to be will!"

I understood now what he meant. However, by going back and convincing myself to make another choice, everything good about my current life would disappear, even the memories. I would never know Aideen, Dani, Liam, Orla, Clarion, Zephyr, or Cabal. I would never meet any of the time links who were now living in 2257 because of what I had done. Aideen and Dani would never meet. Liam and Orla would never become partners, living on a planet I helped to settle. All of the wonderful things that were part of my good/bad existence made Path Three a difficult one to follow. But what about Path Two?

Path Two was the one I had glimpsed during my last few jumps before returning to my living room in Ambleside. A life with Annette, alone in a world empty of all others except the children we bore and the Community of Minds. We would live the life of love and tenderness I had always wished I could have with Annette. And we would have it for hundreds of years before I turned into the Anomaly, far, far more time together than the vast majority of people in Earth's long history had lived, much less spent with the love of their life. With all my being, I thought of it. I cleansed every other thought from my mind. What I coveted was Annette and only Annette. I always had. I couldn't invent a better way to spend several lifetimes with her. All to myself. I would choose Option Two.

And the best thing about that choice was that the mind-reading son of a bitch in front of me actually believed me.

Chapter 28

The Anomaly sent me back to Annette in 2749. She was in the control room of the time station, and that is where I arrived as if he knew that's where she was. I had forgotten about the time camera embedded in the back of my neck—and it's a good thing because then he would have known—but the look in Annette's eyes told me she knew everything.

"Can you take me out of here?" she asked.

"Take my hand, and let's try. We need to move quickly, Annette!"

She picked up a bag lying on the counter beside her, presumably, things she had packed in anticipation of a hasty exit from this reality, then grasped my hand. I thought of the one place I knew better than any other and urged the OIM inside me to calculate a path to take us there. I blacked out for a moment and then regained my senses inside Murphy's pub in 2257. This jump proved it was true that I could move through time on my own and from one reality to another, both of which we had done during this trip. The pub was packed, and all the assorted characters were there. Annette was still with me, holding my hand.

"What have we here?" asked Aideen. "Charles told us about this false reality you were livin' in, Annette, and we got your message that you had it under control, so am I to assume you've broken out of there?"

"We escaped, but there's another problem," said Annette.

Aideen squinted her eyes, sensing trouble. "What might that be?" she asked.

"We're being pursued by the predator who put Annette in the false reality. He's very powerful, and he can transit across time and between realities with the snap of his fingers. He's undoubtedly coming after us as we speak!"

It was probably the look of fear on both of our faces that caused Aideen's expression to change. Dani and Orla approached, as did Clarion and Zephyr, and Liam shuffled down the bar to the spot where Annette and I were standing. He didn't even bother to offer us an ale.

"What's the meanin' of this, Charles?" he asked, his tone serious. "Are you tellin' us the truth?"

"Yes!" I screamed. "And I'm just here to warn you then we've got to keep moving."

I gave a quick summary of what had happened, but I didn't tell them who the Anomaly actually was. The shame of it was too much for me to confess. "I just want you to know that he might be coming here to look for us and possibly to take one or more of you hostage, or worse. I don't know how to stop him, but maybe the force field tech can be adapted somehow. But we've got to leave, now! Annette, think of a place where we can go and think of it very hard. I should be able to pick it up, and we can go there."

Annette reached into her bag and pulled out two pills and two oxygen masks. She swallowed one of the pills and gave one to me. "It's an anti-gravity pill, and it works much faster than the anti-gravity pills from your time. I took the pill. "Now put this on," she said, handing me the mask, then putting the one she had onto her face. It latched on around her nose and mouth. I did the same. "Okay, I'm thinking now of where and when we want to go," she said.

Before I put the mask on, I warned the others again. "Protect yourselves! He's coming! We will return if we survive. I promise."

I put the mask on, grasped Annette's hand while reading her mind, and told the OIM in me to make it happen. Boom!

*****

We materialized on the surface of a planet composed entirely of silver-gray rock. We were on a plain, but I could see vast mountains in the distance. I was breathing through the oxygen mask, but my sophisticated clothing was sending me readings that the surface of this planet was scorching and that the atmosphere was mainly carbon dioxide. Not far away was a city made from the same silvery rock as the land surface. Buildings of different heights and shapes rose toward the sky, and it could have been a city on Earth, except the color was silver-gray, not black. I felt the intense gravity immediately. It was at least twice that of Terrene and three times that of Earth, but the fast-working anti-gravity pill Annette had given me was already compensating, lightening the load I was feeling by strengthening every aspect of my body—bone, tissue, etc., etc.

Thank you for the pills and the mask, I said, using telepathy since we couldn't use our spoken voices in this poisonous atmosphere. *You've been thinking ahead.*

I knew what was coming, she said, alluding to the time camera I'd been transporting in my neck that gave her the story of the Anomaly in real time. *We need to get to that city, Charles. It's not our final destination, but we have to go there to get where we're going.*

Annette moved forward, and I followed. There was no road, but that's because the entire plain was as smooth and hard as a road. Harder, most likely. I had yet to see vegetation of any kind. *What year is this?* I asked.

I was thinking of my most recent visit here, in 2739, so that's probably what year it is, but I'm not sure.

What's the surface of this planet made of? I asked. *Is it iron?*

Yes, that's what I'm told, she said, continuing to press forward.

As we headed toward the city, which now seemed a formidable distance away, I heard a thumping sound, like the sound of someone running on the surface of a drum. It was coming from behind us, so I turned around and saw a massive creature approaching. It was made from the same silver-gray rock as the landscape around us, and it was approximately ten meters tall. It had two legs and two arms, with gigantic hands and a head that sat on a stumpy neck. Its chest was broad and was more than four meters across. As it came closer, Annette filled me in.

This is one of the species that inhabit this planet, she said. *Do you remember the largest eggs you saw at the bottom of the Terrene Ocean?*

Yes, I said, remembering they were at least ten meters tall and five meters wide.

Those eggs contain these beings. They are known, in English, as Ironites since they are basically made of iron, as is the mantle of this entire world. I'll tell you more later, but while these creatures are technically alive, they were manufactured by the beings we are here to see.

The Ironite approaching us slowed down, stopping in front of us. It leaned down, then scooped us up, one of us in each of its massive hands. It began running again toward the city. Annette continued to fill me in on things as we bounced along.

The Ironites are servants of the masters of this planet, which is known as Strata, she said.

Will they protect us? I asked.

They will try, she said. *But it would be better if we made it to our final destination to get full protection.*

We reached the city, which had streets on it but no vehicles. The streets were as wide as a football field, and pedestrians were strolling up and down, more Ironites, but not many of them. I counted maybe a dozen of them as we approached a massive structure at the end of the giant boulevard we were traveling down.

The building ahead is where we need to go, said Annette.

Is that where this thing is taking us? I asked. *How did it know to do that?*

We obviously don't belong here, she said. *It's just trying to take us to its masters.*

Okay.

I had many questions, but this was no time to ask them. The rock monster entered the building through a door that was fifteen meters high and approached a massive reception desk, behind which another one of them sat. It spoke to the receptionist in a language that seemed like a series of clicks, almost like Morse code. The receptionist picked up something that resembled a telephone and made a call, then after a moment, it hung up the phone, emitted a few clicks to the one holding us, and nodded its head. Our captor/savior turned and approached an elevator, which surprised me by going down rather than up. Our transit time was also longer than I expected it would be. Even though the elevator was plummeting fast enough for my ears to pop, it traveled for many minutes before gently coming to a stop deep under the planet's surface.

The huge elevator doors opened onto a vast underground chamber. Two sentinels of some kind were waiting for us there. The Ironite put us down, stepped back into the elevator, and the doors closed, leaving us alone, standing in front of the two sentinels. Annette removed her mask, and I followed her lead, breathing in air rich in oxygen and humidity.

The most astonishing thing about the two beings standing in front of us was their height. They stood only a meter tall, on three legs that fed directly into a large, spherical mass that seemed to contain both brain and whatever other biological components they needed to live. The head/body held several eyes, at least four running around the sphere's equator and one directly on the top. The legs seemed to also function as arms, which became apparent when each of the sentinels raised one leg in the air and gave us some kind of salute.

"These two will take us to the leader of this planet," said Annette.

"How do you know?" I asked.

"Because I just left yesterday," said Annette. "I'm sure they're wondering why I've returned so soon."

Chapter 29

I noticed immediately that the color of the rock down here—gray speckled with red, perhaps red granite—was different from the silver-gray material up above, and I suspected it had something to do with how the planet had been formed billions of years ago. Perhaps the planet had spun so rapidly during its molten phase that heavier materials, like iron, were thrown toward the surface, and the lighter materials, such as granite, remained lower. The red in the rock here was probably oxidized iron, which turned red from the presence of oxygen and water, which were not present in large quantities on the surface. I wondered if Annette had brought us to this planet because of the iron mantle. Perhaps she was thinking it might somehow limit the ability of the Anomaly to travel through it. That might also explain why she brought us to the surface rather than directly to this underground chamber. Because she had no choice.

I was most interested in learning more about where we were now. The cavern seemed nearly a kilometer across, and the domed ceiling was hundreds of meters above us. A light shone down from above and was obviously of the kind that could grow plants because the whole place was inundated with fauna and various types of trees, similar to the jungles of Earth, but with leaves and trunks of a variety of colors, including yellow, red and purple. I could feel the humidity in the air on my face, obviously created and sustained by the plants. The oxygen in the air seemed quite rich due to the plant life. I assumed the walls of the complex sealed everything in, so it was likely relatively easy to sustain. Multi-level towers, made of some other yellowish material, rose high into the air throughout the chamber, open for the eye to see in and occupied by thousands of the little tripod beings like the ones that were now leading us forward.

"This is mostly a government administrative facility," Annette clarified. "The leaders also work here. The English translation for this species is 'Troglodytes' because they live underground, not because it's what they call themselves. There are gaps in the translation software that enables us to communicate with them. You see, they speak that same clicking language used by the Ironites. It makes sense that since the Troglodytes created the Ironites, they would have them speak their language."

"What is the purpose of the Ironites?" I asked.

"They mine and guard the surface," said Annette. "Iron is in short supply in this star system. Species from other planets in the system have tried to mine the surface, so the Troglodytes created the Ironites to keep the aliens from stealing their iron, and now that they mine the iron themselves, it's become a lucrative export for this planet."

We were led to a structure similar to the others but only about thirty meters high. We boarded a lift that took us to the top, and we disembarked on the highest floor, which was literally the roof of the building. Around a dozen desks were scattered around the area, each with a tripod standing behind it. From what I could see, these beings didn't sit, couldn't sit, actually. Many of them were relying solely on one leg to hold them upright, with the other two manipulating machines, probably computers, that sat on their desks. One of them stepped away from their station and scurried toward us. I noticed for the first time that the toes on their circular feet were doing the walking. I counted twelve toes per foot, each in a vertical position, marching in rapid mini-steps as would the legs of a centipede. The toes were about six inches long and could function as fingers, too, since they had two or three joints in them.

The creature approached us, and I could see that it was carrying a rectangular device of some kind, probably the translation unit. It clicked a few things into the box through a mouth that shared the top of its head with the centrally located eye. The translation unit spoke to us in stilted English, suggesting the technology of these beings was less advanced than Earth's. "Hello, Annette. Why have you returned so quickly? Is something wrong?"

Annette introduced me first, telling the tripod my name and then telling me that this one was called Cassandra in English. You have to understand that these names I'm giving you are simply conveniences we humans use, so we can refer to aliens as something other than "tripod" or "alien." I mean, here is this alien, telling us its name is "Click, Click, Click," and that comes out of the machine as "Cassandra." The reality is that the creature is named "Click, Click, Click," but the software has to give it a name we can relate to, so it does, and I have no idea how it makes its choice other than to make sure it doesn't give out the same name twice.

The creature lifted one of its feet up and shook my hand. Its toes/fingers enveloped my outstretched hand since the diameter of the foot/hand was greater than the width of my hand. I wondered about the protocol for cleanliness in this world since only seconds previously, the fingers that were now touching mine were creeping along the floor, which, although it looked clean, must have contained any number of particles of dirt and germs.

Annette must have seen the expression on my face because she clarified the situation. "The material that these structures are made of absorbs any foreign particles that fall onto it. This is the most sanitary place you can imagine."

"Is the material alive?" I asked. "Like OIM?"

"I don't think so," said Annette. "Its ability to absorb particles is inherent to its nature."

I don't know what that meant, but we had more pressing matters to discuss, so I let it go. Annette explained to the leader of the Troglodytes what was going on, that she was actually Annette from 2749, that we were very likely being pursued by an aggressive being with bad intentions, and that we were seeking protection from the monster. Unfortunately, the response from Cassandra that came out of the translation box wasn't what we had wanted to hear.

"I've just received word that the creature you speak of is already on the surface, doing battle with the Ironites."

Chapter 30

"Do the Ironites have brains?" I asked.

"Yes," said Annette. "Small ones. But if you're thinking Bad Charles can use mind-control on them, it's not likely. Those creatures are as close to solid iron as a living thing can get, and I don't believe he'll be able to penetrate their skulls and get to the brain. The fact that he's on the surface supports my theory that iron limits all his powers, including time travel, molecular reconstruction travel, and mind control. He can't get through iron!"

"That's a good start, but he's here anyway. Well, up there. What is he fighting them with if he doesn't have mind control as an option?"

Annette took a moment to ask Cassandra what was transpiring on the surface, then the answer issued forth from the translation box. "The intruder has a hand-held laser. The Ironites have force fields that can deflect the laser, and they are shooting at him with their canons, but he disappears before the projectile hits him, then reappears in another place. He doesn't seem to know exactly where to go, but he is already in the city, and since the building with the elevator is the largest, most prominent building in the city, he will most likely go there."

"Do we have any weapons down here?" I asked.

The translation box said, "There is no need for weapons down here."

I thought this through and requested two things: first, I asked if Cassandra could bring a contingent of Ironites down the elevator before the Anomaly reached it to stand guard here in the underground city; second, I asked if there was an escape route we could follow that would allow us to get back to the surface and transport ourselves to another place and time. The answer was yes, to both questions.

Annette apologized to Cassandra for putting her in danger, but Cassandra didn't seem to mind. She said they would tell the creature you were gone if it broke through defenses and could ride the elevator down.

"Can't you just shut the elevator off?" I asked.

"We can," said the voice from the translation device. "But the shaft is still there, and this creature could simply burn through the iron floor of the elevator and transport itself here. You should get moving right away."

A flying vehicle of some kind arrived beside the roof and hovered there, waiting for us. It was long and slender, like a cigar, and it appeared we would have to crawl on board and lie on our stomachs to use it.

"My apologies," said Cassandra, but we don't build vehicles for humans here yet. The visits are so few and far between, you see."

"It's no problem," said Annette, reaching forward and touching Cassandra on her colossal head. "Thank you for your help, Cassandra. I hope the trouble we brought on you comes to a quick close when we leave."

"I'm sure it will," she said, handing Annette a small box. "This device will allow us to stay in communication until you leave the planet. Good luck to you both! Goodbye, Annette. Goodbye, Charles."

I waved goodbye, walked over to the vehicle, got on my knees, crawled in through a door opening just over one-meter high, then riggled toward the front to make room for Annette. She entered, the door slid shut, and the vehicle departed. There didn't seem to be a driver, but it had likely already been programmed on where to go. It flew forward, negotiating around the various structures in the great cavern, and ultimately approached a hole in the wall that was surprisingly small, with a diameter of perhaps three meters. Immediately upon entering the tunnel, everything outside became dark. Annette and I had lowered ourselves flat onto the floor and had our arms and legs stretched out to make contact with the walls to stabilize ourselves. I had noticed upon entry that looped handles came down from the ceiling, as would be the case on a subway, undoubtedly for the tripods to hold on to while they stood in the bus.

There were very few turns, which was good because that would have had deleterious effects on our gastrointestinal integrity. I had no idea how fast we were traveling, but we sped forward for nearly an hour. Finally, we emerged from the dark into another vast chamber similar to the one we'd been in previously. The bus lowered itself to the floor in front of a huge elevator like the one before. One of the Ironites was there waiting for us. The elevator doors opened, but Annette made contact with Cassandra before stepping on. I waited to hear the translation come through. "He has entered the shaft of the elevator."

"How did he break through?" asked Annette.

"He's found a way to cause the Ironites to break apart, leaving only a pile of ashes behind!"

I knew what that was. It was an old OIM trick of mine, used for the first time when Aideen, Dani, and I destroyed Diaspora One.

"He's here!" screamed Cassandra. "Go! Now!"

"Tell him which way we went!" screamed Annette. "Perhaps that will keep him from harming you. It won't matter to our fate. We are leaving your planet in minutes. He will follow us, I'm sure."

The three of us stepped on board the elevator. The doors closed, and we shot toward the surface. While riding up, Annette and I put on our oxygen masks. When we arrived, the doors opened, and we looked out upon a vast wasteland. There was no city, no buildings, except the elevator housing itself. In the distance, there were signs of mining activity but nothing else. Now was the time to go before the Anomaly figured out where we were. Annette was one step ahead of me, reaching for my hand and nodding at me, telling me to bore into her mind and establish the coordinates for our next destination. I did so, and soon after that, everything went blank.

Chapter 31

When I regained my senses, I was still holding Annette's hand but was confused about what kind of place we'd arrived at. The surface I was standing on was solid and flat, but it was perfectly smooth and looked to be made from some type of light metal, perhaps aluminum. The edge of the platform looked to be circular. I released Annette's hand and initiated a slow swivel, following the border around and confirming that it was a circle. We were standing on a disk with a diameter of twenty-five or thirty meters. I also felt very light; I don't know why, but presumably because this place had a much lower gravity than Terrene, even lower than Earth's. Much lower. I felt so light that if a mild wind came along, it might blow us off the disk.

Annette took my hand again and led me to the edge of the disk. "Be very careful as we look over the edge, all right?"

I nodded my head and stretched it out so I could see over and what I saw caused me to jerk back and move away from the edge. It was the feeling one would have when looking down the side of a cliff, similar to what all of us back on Terrene felt when we looked over the immense and spectacular cliffs of New Madagascar, peering down one thousand meters to the sea below us. But what I had seen when I looked down from the edge of the disk resembled some kind of endless drop, as far as the eye could see. I literally could see no ground below us. The clear air at our elevation eventually gave way to thin, white clouds below, but they were far below us.

"Are we up in the atmosphere of this planet?" I asked.

"Yes," she replied. "This is a moon, actually, of a gas giant in the habitable zone of a star system that's tens of thousands of light-years from Earth. It's known on Earth as Olympia, but the inhabitants, known by us as Avioids, call it something else. I just can't pronounce it. I've been here only once, and it was my last stop on a very long string of diplomatic visits. The year of my visit was 2298, only one year before I retired. It was a long time ago for me."

"It has a breathable atmosphere," I said. "Even though the gravity feels like it's one-fifth of the gravity on Terrene and therefore only about one-third of the gravity on Earth. How is that possible?"

"The moon itself has low metal content compared to most planets and moons, and this lowers its gravity, and coupled with its small size, the gravity is only about 30 percent that of Earth's. Far more gas escapes from the atmosphere here than on Earth or Terrene. But there is healthy volcanic activity down below, which replaces the gas, and apparently, the proximity to the gas giant has helped sustain the volcanic activity longer than a small planet like this should be able to do. There is liquid water below, on the surface, because we are in the habitable zone of this star system. The Oxygen, Nitrogen proportions are similar to Earth's, with a healthy layer of CO_2 above us, deflecting the rays from the sun, which helps limit the escape of Oxygen by cooling the upper atmosphere while helping the lower altitudes retain heat."

"Well, well, Annette. You have become quite the astrophysicist in your role as head of interstellar space exploration."

Annette smiled, seemingly appreciating the compliment. "Thank you, Charles."

"Getting back to the issue at hand, however, what is to keep the Anomaly from finding us here? Did I tell you that's what I'm calling that thing, by the way?"

"I could think of other things to call it, but fine," she said. "Anyway, other than it being a long way from Earth and from Strata, I'm not sure what will keep him from finding us. But hopefully, he can't fly."

Just as I began to ask about how we were going to fly, even in this low-gravity environment, two winged creatures landed on the disk. They were four-legged beasts, but they didn't have hooves. They had feet that looked like hands, each with four fingers, and when they landed, they stood up on two hind legs and folded their wings behind themselves. Oh, and I just remembered. They were approximately three times as tall as humans when they stood on their hind legs. Their heads were blocky, shaped like a cube with rounded edges, and they had two eyes and two ears, a mouth, but no nose. The teeth in their mouths were sharp and pointed, like vampire's teeth; only all of them were that way. They also had long slits along their necks that might be gills. Perhaps these avian creatures were also water creatures. Their appendages were long, thin, and wiry, with two elbows. Their color was a brilliant orange. They were each carrying something, and when they came close to us, they placed the two packages onto the floor of the disk.

One of them spoke to us in perfect, unaccented English. "Hello, Annette. We weren't expecting you, but we are happy to see you. It wasn't long ago, during your visit, that you said you would try your best to return, but so soon! We are happy."

"Thank you, Didimeen. My companion is named Charles, and I am sorry to inform you that we are being pursued by a malicious being who means us harm."

"Can it fly?" asked Didimeen.

"I'm hoping it can't," said Annette. "But we must hurry. We don't want to be here when he arrives."

Annette reached out and began unpacking one of the packages. It contained a pair of wings, and Didimeen approached her and helped her attach them to both of her arms. The other Avioid helped me unpack my wings and secured them onto my arms. At that point, something miraculous occurred. The straps simply melted into my skin and flesh, and the wings molded themselves around my arms, becoming a part of my body.

Just then, the Anomaly appeared on the far side of the disk and charged toward us.

"Come on!" screamed Annette, rushing toward the edge of the disk. "Jump! And fly!"

Annette jumped off the disk and flapped her wings, putting some distance between herself and me, but she remained at a level where she could see what was happening. The two Avioids took flight, leaving me alone on the platform, and I was simply too terrified to jump off. The Anomaly caught me, holding onto me tightly.

"You always were afraid of heights, Charles," he said. "Come, let me take you somewhere where you can't make trouble. I'll return later to gather up Annette.

Was she so foolish as to think I couldn't grow wings in an instant?"

Just as the Anomaly was about to abscond with me, to place me in some other reality or some such place, the Avioids attacked. They attacked with sound. It was a piercing, high-pitched whistle sound, and I felt as if my head would explode. Within seconds, I blacked out.

Chapter 32

I opened my eyes. I was lying in a bed that seemed twice as large as a normal one, and then I remembered where I was. The creatures who lived here in Olympia, the Avioids, were much larger than humans. Apparently, they had rescued me from the Anomaly and brought me here. I looked up and saw the ceilings were far above me, also to accommodate the tremendous height of these beings, especially when they stood on two legs. Annette was standing by the bed, holding my hand. A wave of emotion crashed through me.

"What happened?" I asked.

"The Avioids were able to subdue the Anomaly with their sonic weapons. He was out long enough for them to encase him in a strong container they otherwise use to hold their enemies from other parts of Olympia. It's a clear but very robust material, enabling them to watch him inside the container. Not long after, he woke up and disappeared. Presumably, he is preparing himself to withstand the sonic blasts that deterred his last effort. How are you feeling, Charles?"

I noticed Annette was still holding my hand (how could I not!) and relished every second of it. "I'm feeling okay," I told her, even though my head was pounding from the sonic blast that had disabled me. I wouldn't want to go through that again. As I looked closer at Annette, I noticed the wings that had been fused to her arms were gone, and I reached to feel for mine. Gone as well. "So we won't be needing the wings anymore?" I asked.

"We need to leave this place quickly," she said. "It seems that nothing we try is enough to outrun your future self. I have no reason to believe that what he said isn't true. That he can grow wings if he wants to and perhaps even fly using other methods. He'll be back as soon as he figures out a way to defend himself against the sonic weapons. We have to be gone by then."

"Do the Avioids have any other weapons to slow him down?"

"Not that I'm aware of. The sonic blasts are effective against their enemies, and they also use them to hunt for food in the ocean down below. They primarily eat seafood."

"Is there land down there?"

"Yes, and that is where their enemies live. It's another intelligent race, some kind of quadruped, like themselves. I've never seen them, but I hear they are vicious and have some rudimentary flying technology that allows them to ascend up here and attack the Avioids."

"Where is here, exactly?" I asked.

"We're in the capital city of Olympia," she said. "It floats high up in the air, like the landing pad we used, based on some kind of levitation tech the Avioids developed. I'd like to show you around because it's quite an amazing place, but we really have to go, Charles. Are you able to get up and move around?"

"Yes, of course," I said. "But where are we going? It seems we can't get away from him no matter where we go?"

Just then, the Avioid named Didimeen entered the room. He was walking on all fours, so he wasn't as intimidatingly tall, but he was still at least a meter taller than Annette as she stood by my bedside. "How are you, Charles?" he asked.

"Much better," I said. "Thank you for rescuing me."

"It is our pleasure. That fellow looked quite dangerous and seemed to intend you harm."

It appeared that Annette had not yet explained to the Avioids that the "fellow" Didimeen had referenced was me, and I saw no need to get into that.

"Actually, my friend, I think it was Annette he meant to harm, but you saved us so that matter is handled for now."

"Yes," said Annette. "And to prevent further disruptions to your world, we should be leaving right away."

"You think this troublemaker will return?" he asked.

"We do," she said. "And he will have very likely developed the ability to resist your sonic weapons and come prepared to fly, too. Do you have any other weapons that might dissuade him?"

"We do," said Didimeen. "We are not concerned."

"Best to just tell him we've moved on," I said. "To places unknown to you, which will be true. He'll leave to follow us at that point."

"We wish you well, then," he said.

I raised up out of bed and experienced a wave of nausea, but suppressed it and got myself to my feet. "Do you have any ideas, Annette, of where we might go to evade the beast?'

"I have one more thing we need to try," she said. "Are you ready?"

"Of course," I said, even though I felt worse than I could ever remember since I'd taken the immunity pills long ago.

Annette took my hand. "Thank you, Didimeen, for helping us."

"Good luck to you both," he said.

Annette concentrated on the new destination, and I commanded the OIM inside me to take us there. We popped out of existence on Olympia, presumably on the way to the next place Annette had in mind.

Chapter 33

I regained consciousness and found myself alone, floating inside what appeared to be a cloud. My feet weren't touching the ground, but it was different than the feeling of weightlessness. I could feel the weight of my body, and there was a sensation of falling, no, not exactly that. It felt like I should be falling, but something, perhaps someone, was holding me up.

The fog surrounded me on all sides, and as I thought about it, I realized Annette could be nearby since I could only see a few feet in front of me.

"Annette?" I called out. "Annette! Are you here?"

Silence. I swiveled in a circle and continued to shout for Annette. Whatever was holding me up wasn't letting go yet. But Annette wasn't nearby; if she was, she couldn't communicate with me, either with the spoken voice or telepathically. For all intents and purposes, I was alone. I waited there for a while, how long I don't know, periodically calling Annette's name to see if circumstances had changed. But I did not see or hear Annette, and as it turned out, I didn't have contact with her the entire time I was in that place. I wondered if the Anomaly had intercepted us and put me there and Annette somewhere else. I worried that he might hurt her.

Suddenly, I began to move in a horizontal direction. The fog was thick, and I could feel it passing over me and into my lungs as I breathed. I wasn't moving quickly, perhaps as fast as a brisk walking pace, and then I came up against a black wall. I knew what the wall was made of, but it didn't speak to me when I addressed it telepathically. I touched the wall, and an opening appeared. I stepped through it and found myself in a black and seemingly endless hallway. There was no fog in here, and as I turned around, I saw that the opening I had come in through had sealed up. I turned back to face the hallway and could not see the end of it. Perhaps it genuinely was endless.

I walked down the hallway, and from time to time, I would touch the walls to see if they would create an opening for me, but they remained solid. I walked and walked and walked. For hours I trudged forward. I walked for such a long time that I actually developed a thirst, which was soon followed by hunger. Was this some kind of hell I'd been put in, my fate simply to walk forever down this passageway with no water and no food until I expired. Or was I already dead and actually would do this forever. Just walk down an empty hallway for eternity.

Finally, the hallway ended (you guessed it) at a black wall. I touched the wall, and it opened. In front of me was…a conference room. It was a duplicate of the one Annette and I had been meeting in at the Space Exploration complex in 2749. The comfortable chairs were there, and a full glass of red wine was sitting next to one of them. I assumed this meant I was to sit there, so I did. I really didn't want the wine at the moment. What I wanted was water. Suddenly, a glass of water sprouted from the table. I snatched it up and sucked it down like a man in the desert who'd just found an oasis. I set the water down, and the glass disappeared into the table, only to be replaced by another, replenished with more delicious water. I took it in my hand and drank a few more sips, then set it down and reached for the wine. As I sipped the delicious Pinot Noir, I thought of food, and a plate of crisps and hummus—one of my favorites—appeared. I munched on the food as politely as possible, wondering who I might be trying to placate with some semblance of manners, when a voice came into my head.

Hello Charles, said the voice.

I was frustrated that this was Annette's voice, doubting very much that it was her because the tone was one of omnipotence, and that was not a tone Annette ever used, even though she probably had some basis for doing so during her illustrious career.

You are correct that we are not Annette, but it seemed an excellent choice to help you feel more comfortable during your stay here, which we assure you will be brief.

Do you want me to speak using telepathy or with my voice? I asked.

Your choice, came the response.

"I think I'll use my real voice, then," I said. Somehow using my physical voice made me feel more comfortable at that moment, more human, because, very likely, whatever I was speaking to was not human unless it was the Anomaly impersonating Annette.

No, we are not your future self, Charles. And yes, we are not human.

"What are you then?" I asked.

We are a collection of sorts. A collection of intelligent species.

Of course, I wanted to know more, but there was also the matter of Annette.

"Where is Annette?" I asked. "The real Annette."

She is being held in stasis, back on Earth, and we've stopped time there until you rejoin her.

Well, that was quite a trick if it was true. Stopping time was something I'd never even considered, and I wondered how they did that.

One day you will learn the answer to that query, Charles.

"How?" I asked.

Because one day soon, you will join us. Actually, you have already joined us because time is not linear here. For us, this meeting has already taken place, but you must experience it in linear time in order to end up here permanently.

"Why? How?"

The why is that we want you to join us. We said we are a collection, remember? A collection of what remains of living things from throughout the galaxy when their biological status ends. But only some living things come here. Only the ones we choose.

"You mean when they die, right? Is that what you're saying? Are you God?"

When they die, yes. The part about God is fluid, however. We serve as God when the need arises. On Terrene, for example, we serve as the Watcher from the Sky.

"Wait, I thought Annette was the Watcher from the Sky?"

She is, but her chicken-egg theory is flawed. She has simply been repeating the process that we had already initiated. As you know, Charles, time repeats itself. The past, present, and future are happening simultaneously, forever.

As you might suspect, I had dozens of questions percolating in my mind, and I wanted to ask all of them, but this being, this collection of beings, didn't seem to have that in its plans.

Charles, you will learn all the answers when you come to us permanently. For now, we should say that while we want good things to happen for the living beings in the galaxy, we can only tamper with things so much. Otherwise, we might upset the circle of life. Again, more will become apparent to you soon. We brought you here while you are still alive simply to tell you that this Anomaly of yours has become too powerful. He is in a position to upset the circle of life in the galaxy in ways that we cannot repair. We are not all-powerful, Charles. We can exert influence, yes, but we never should have released the secret of time travel to your Community of Minds. We thought it was a logical next step after the Minds were given OIM and after the humans made such good use of it to create peace and harmony on your planet, with one exception, I might add—you. But biological beings are too...limited to manage the power of time travel. Humans were the best hope for it to work, but ultimately, they failed. Time travel, and its cousin, reality travel, should remain with us outside the biological realm. Unfortunately, we are having difficulty making that happen because of your future self, Charles.

My mind was spinning with all the information pouring into it. Apparently, this "Collection" had given OIM, then time travel, to the Minds, but did the Minds know that, or were they made to believe they had invented those things on their own? But the Collection wouldn't stop to let me think, and it kept dumping information into me, and I couldn't stop it.

Charles, you are not so unlike many beings in the galaxy. You are filled with the potential to do good and also with the potential to do evil. But this Anomaly has taken over your future and must be dealt with. You are the only one with the power to do so. We brought you here to urge you to act.

"I can't stop him!" I screamed. "That's why I'm running from him!"

There was no immediate answer from the Collection, and finally, I had time to think. It was all beginning to make sense, but just then, it ended our conversation.

Say nothing of this to Annette, or anyone else, Charles. You know what you have to do. We await your arrival.

Chapter 34

I materialized back in the control room of the time station on Earth, holding hands with Annette. There was no momentary lapse of clarity as would happen with a typical time jump, at least for me, but Annette seemed a little woozy, probably because she'd been held in time stasis for a while and was just coming out of it. I had to accept that I now had a secret to keep unless what I'd just experienced was simply a dream or a hallucination. But it didn't matter. The Anomaly was still after us, and we certainly weren't protected at our current location. He visited this place all the time. I needed to act quickly. The first step was regaining my bearings. From Annette's point of view, we had just come here from Olympia in 2298. I wondered when we were.

"What year is this, Annette?"

"It's 2749, moments after we departed for Terrene," she said.

"Why here?"

"We have to find a way to get him off our trail," she said.

"What do you have in mind?" I asked.

"Let's use the time station. He seems to be tracking where you go based on however it is you get the OIM to take you there. You have to communicate with it, right, to get it to transport you?"

"Yes, but this time station is also made of OIM. He can simply ask it where and when we went, and it will tell him."

"The Minds can help us!" she said. "They can communicate with the OIM too and feed it false information."

"I don't know," I said. "I just don't know."

"Look, Charles, I've worked exclusively with the Minds for eight years, doing things that were never done before, and I know what the Minds can do. The power of a hundred million brains can wipe the memory of the OIM here in the station clean and put other information in its place. I know it can work!"

"Then do it!" I said.

Annette approached the console that apparently facilitated communication with the Minds. It made sense that it was in the control room, but I'd never seen it used. Direct contact with the Minds had always been strictly controlled, and relatives were never allowed to speak with their kin that had gone into the Community. This way, the decision to become a Mind was serious because even though the individual would have an entirely new and fulfilling life, to the biological friends and family they left behind, it was the equivalent of losing them by death. That is why everyone on Terrene was so sad when they heard that Danielle and Aideen's clone had become Minds. No one would ever see or hear from them again.

But Annette had been in charge of human contact with the Minds for over one hundred years and had a lifetime authorization to communicate with them. She pushed a button on the console and spoke as if she were addressing another human being. "Hello, this is Annette, as I'm sure you know. I am seeking contact with the Administrative Coordinator, who I believe is Daniel Mubarri. May I speak with him, please? The matter is urgent."

A response came immediately from the speaker on the console. "How can I help you, Annette."

"More trouble from time travel, I'm afraid," she said. She briefly explained what was going on and her plan to evade the Anomaly. After she finished speaking, there was a slight pause, then Mubarri's voice came over the speaker.

"The Minds are concerned that this Anomaly might destroy the monolith if he suspects our involvement," he said.

"I can't make any guarantees," said Annette. "I can only tell you that this is a separate reality and that the

Minds live on in many other realities. As you know, the only biological human here has been me for eight years until Charles arrived. But I can't make you do this, as I have no guarantees as to what the Anomaly might do. I would say, however, that if you properly reprogram the OIM in this station, he would have no reason to suspect you. And again, the Minds live on in numerous other realities. I assure you the Minds will continue on, no matter what happens here."

After another slight delay, Mubarri spoke. "Very well, we'll take care of it. I suggest you move quickly to exit this time and place."

"Thank you, Daniel. The Minds are dear friends." Annette pushed the button to shut down communication with the Minds, a control I was sure was responsive only to her touch, and a handful of other biological humans. She rushed over to the time station console and programmed something in. "It's set to send us in one minute. Let's get down into the station."

We entered the station, and Annette took my hand. "I hope this works," she said.

"Me too," I replied. Then we flashed out of consciousness, regaining our senses in the living room of my old penthouse apartment on the top floor of the OIMtech headquarters when I was CEO and majority stockholder of the company. The floor-to-ceiling windows of the circular apartment, up on the 49th floor, had a panoramic view of London. It was breathtaking, but I must tell you that I did not relish the idea of being there. "What year is this?" I asked Annette.

"It's 2183," said Annette. "Time travel has just been invented by the Community of Minds. You and I are deeply in love, and you've not yet informed me of your decision to steal the time travel tech."

"Why are we here, Annette?"

"You know why, Charles. It's the Anomaly's Option Three. The one where you decide not to steal the time travel tech after all. The one where you and I can be together, in love, forever."

"I suppose the two of us are right through that door, in the bedroom?" I asked, dipping my head toward the door in question.

"Making love for the last time," she said. "In the reality that came to pass when you informed me of your plan to steal the time travel tech. In fact, I think you'll tell me in about thirty minutes, after we shower together and get ready for work. It's a memory I will never forget, Charles."

I have to tell you, I could not believe what I was hearing from Annette. Did she still love me? Did she still want to spend her life with me? After all of these hundreds of years, all of my dastardly deeds, and all of her fabulous accomplishments, she still loved me? I had to know.

"Annette, right now, here in this room, our living room, not there in our bedroom, do you still love me?"

She didn't hesitate. "I do, Charles. I love you with all my heart and have never loved another, never even had another lover. It was either going to be you, or it was going to be no one. I love you, and I want us to be together. But only this way. Only the right way."

And now it was up to me.

Chapter 35

When the Anomaly presented me with the three paths my life could take, I evaluated each in turn. Path One was to do nothing. Continue on as I was and ultimately become him. That would be a difficult choice, knowing that my evil side would win out in the end. Path Two was to go to the reality created by my future evil self and live the rest of my days with Annette, walking the streets of a world that belonged to us. The problem, of course, was that it would only be us. We would have our pet wolves and bears and other animals I could control with my mind, and we would have children, too, apparently. But would you want to have children if there were no others for them to share the world with? I don't think so. And then there was Path Three. Right here. Right now. I was in a position to right every wrong I'd ever made and to be with the person I loved more than any other, and she had just told me that I was the love of her life. The only love of her life. How could I not take that path?

"Annette," I said. "If you only knew how long I have waited to hear you say those words again. Hearing those words has been my life's goal since I broke the OIM addiction and regained my sanity. I realize that when I tell you, over there in the bedroom, of my selfish plan, it ruined our life together and the lives of those I killed and their families. You know I have wanted to correct that more than anything else."

"And now I have brought you to the place where that can happen, Charles." Annette reached out and touched my shoulder, and I swooned. If there was a God, I would have begged him to give me the strength to resist her touch to think clearly and do the right thing. But what was the right thing?

"Annette," I pleaded. "Are you sure you've thought this through? Have you thought about all the good we've done, all the good people we've met, and loved, in this life? The life of the two of us standing here in this living room. The life that those two in the bedroom will lead if we don't open that door. Have you thought about Dani, Aideen, Orla, Liam, Clarion, Zephyr, Cabal, and all the Cassandras and Didimeens of the galaxy that you've met and become friends with? Have you thought about the fact that peace reins throughout the galaxy? Have you thought about your brilliant career? All the firsts you've achieved for the world, for the galaxy?"

Tears streamed down Annette's face, but she had more ammunition, even as she clung tightly to my shoulder, bending me to her will with her touch and her logic. "Charles, he will kill me if he catches us. You know that, don't you? He can't kill you because if he does, he'll be killing himself. But he can take the ones you love. And he will do it! He may have already done it back on Terrene. We have to end this now, Charles, and we're running out of time. Maybe fifteen minutes is all we have for you to walk in there, explain who you are, take younger Charles for a short stroll, and explain to him what will happen if he tells me about his plan and if he proceeds with it. Make him see Charles. I know you can do it!"

I lowered my head, crying, shaking my head, still feeling the caress of Annette's beautiful hand on my shoulder. "Annette, I love you. I've always loved you and always will. And I love what you and I have accomplished, separately and together. And then there are our friends. I know you love them as much as I do. It's too much, Annette! Too much good! I don't want to undo all the good we've done, despite my wrongdoing. I can't! Please!"

"You're not saving us, Charles. You're condemning us to death."

STEVEN DECKER

She tried to pull away, but before she could, I reached up and clasped her hand underneath my own, squeezing tightly, holding her hand in my iron grip. And I thought of home.

Chapter 36

We appeared directly inside Murphy's pub. The year was 2257, and it was the same evening Annette and I had been there before we departed for Strata. Probably three hours later, reflecting in real time how long we'd been gone on our little adventure trying to evade my vicious self. But we had actually been gone longer than that, considering the hours I had been occupied with the Collection while Annette was held in time stasis. And since Annette didn't even know she'd been frozen in time for several hours, coupled with the fact that I'd been sworn to secrecy by the Collection, I just made time pass the way Annette perceived it to be passing.

I was pleased to see that all of my friends were there, apparently unharmed, and I wondered if the Anomaly had even been there, but that matter was quickly clarified by none other than "Miss Up Front and Personal," Aideen.

"Your big brother's been here three times already, Charles!" she said.

"And what a buzz kill that is!" Liam complained. "Bad for business it is, I'll tell you that. A huge black monster of a man pops in, looks around, then pops out. I'm tellin' you, Charles, this has got to come to an end."

"Oh, it will," I said, letting go of Annette's hand, glancing at her and seeing that she was perturbed. Probably a lot more than that, if I'm honest. "I have a plan."

"What?" asked Annette. "Please fill us all in, Charles, because we're running out of options."

"Party at my house!" I yelled.

I looked around and saw the confusion on everyone's face, but I carried on. "It's a beautiful evening, folks, and everyone would readily admit that the view from my backyard is considerably better than it is here. So let's grab a few kegs and a few bottles of Irish whiskey and enjoy the sunset. Then we'll come back here and carry on."

"And what about that big palooka keeps poppin' in and out?" asked Liam. "I thought he was trying to chase you down, Charles?"

"I just remembered there's something at my house that will keep him away from us."

"What?" asked Annette, tilting her head.

"Come with me, and you'll find out."

"Oh, what the feck!" said Liam, hoisting a keg up onto his shoulder. "A few of ye strong folk, give me a hand with a keg or two, will ya'? And everyone brings their glass with them!"

Liam headed for the door, and the clientele of Murphy's pub poured out behind him. The crowd of nearly a hundred strong paraded down the black streets of New Madagascar, passing by the Medical facility where Aideen's clone had been made, the Administrative building where Clarion and Zephyr worked, and eventually made it to my cottage, which sat near the edge of the cliffs about a kilometer out of town. We went around back into my spacious backyard. Liam got the kegs going, I directed my OIM house to pump some Irish music out back, and the party started to rock. The view was spectacular. The cliffs to the east curled out in front of us, giving way to the sea a thousand meters below. It was nearly 14 p.m., and the sun was dropping and would soon plunge into the ocean. I noticed a hovercraft coming toward us from the east, and when it set down in my front yard, I realized who it must be.

Cabal came around back, using his motorized locomotion system, and complaining that he couldn't wait to get the operation that would give him legs, which had been scheduled for a few months hence. He gave me a big bear hug, and we toasted. I didn't dare mention to him that standing right beside me was the "Watcher from the Sky" herself, or at least the latest edition. Annette stood by and kept her mouth shut because, as far she knew, she was the real deal and was obviously uncomfortable standing next to her biggest fan, Cabal. The Collection had claimed that it was the real Watcher from the Sky and had somehow manipulated Annette into performing the miracles witnessed by Land People and Water People thirty thousand years previously, as part of some grand scheme to improve both of the species and to sprinkle some red hot technology into the galaxy. I remember how astonished I had been when I first witnessed the monstrous OIM factory that was spitting out clones and TT modules fifty thousand meters beneath the surface of Terrene's ocean. But now, after the places I'd been and the things I'd witnessed since that memorable trip in Cabal's deep-water sub, that event became just a tiny link in a galaxy-wide chain built by the Collection. Apparently, it played God where and when necessary to tweak the galaxy in the right direction. Perhaps they'd even done so on Earth. They'd admitted to giving the secrets of OIM and time travel to the Community of Minds, so who was to say what they might have done back when all the hot religions came in vogue back in the first millennium of the planet I was born on.

But now was not the time to speculate on such grand matters. Supposedly, I would be filled in on everything if I did what the Collection asked me to do. And as far as the issue at hand went, I realized we were running out of time before "you know who" paid us a visit, and yes, it was a lie I had told to all my friends at Murphy's about there being something here at my home that would keep him away. Well, maybe a white lie, but not wholly untrue. At any rate, there was one person I needed to see before he came, and that was Dani. I left Annette stumbling for words to say to Cabal and went looking for Dani. I found her near one of the kegs, speaking with Zephyr and Clarion, probably her two best friends on Terrene, other than Miss Aideen herself. I approached Dani and asked for a moment of her time, pulling her aside.

"What's up, Charles?" she asked. "You look a little worried. I thought we were protected from your future self here."

"Well, that was a bit of a stretch, but I'm sure everyone will be okay. Say, Dani, I wanted to tell you something. I've been writing a book!"

"Oh really!" she said. "What's it about?"

"It's about my life, the good and the bad, and all of the people I love, like you."

I saw the impact my last statement had on Dani. Her smile turned down into a frown because she knew then that something was up. Dani was the most intelligent person I knew, other than myself and Annette. And in some ways, she was smarter than both of us. She had an intuition that Annette and I lacked. So did

Aideen. But when you mixed the four of us up together, it was pretty strong stuff. We had accomplished a lot as a team. But I digress. Dani was upset.

"Charles, you've never said you loved me, or anyone else, for that matter, at least that I've heard. What gives?'

"Well, you'd be surprised how much I've been using that word over the last few days, Dani, but that's not why I pulled you over here. I've been writing this book, and I have it stored inside my brain, but I'd like to send the file to your handy if you don't mind."

Of course, this comment upset Dani even further. "Why Charles? Why don't you make your own backup disk?"

At that moment, I saw the Anomaly appear on the far side of my yard, not far from where Annette and Cabal were standing. He went directly toward Annette, and I knew the time had come for me to fish or cut bait, so to speak. As my final words as a biological being, I say to you then that I am sorry for the many bad things I've done but proud of the good that resulted from the path I chose.

"Dani, I'm sending it to your handy now!" I said. "Promise me you'll finish it for me!"

*****

"I promise, Charles. But is there no other way?"

"This is the best way, Dani. I know it in my heart."

Charles turned away from me and ran toward the edge of the cliff. I knew what he was going to do, so I screamed the first thing that came into my mind. "You're a good person, Charles!" He didn't turn back, but I believe to this day that he heard me. I watched in horror as he threw himself over the edge. I had seen the Anomaly arrive because I'd felt the time jump, then looked around and spotted him. The Anomaly had gone directly to Annette, grabbed her with one of his monstrous hands, and was dragging her toward the cliff when Charles went over. I imagined a thousand-meter fall would take a few seconds, but before the Anomaly got to the cliff's edge, with Annette fighting him every step of the way, they both disappeared, and I knew then that Charles was dead.

Epilogue

I've read Charles's book, which he called *Addicted to Time,* and I learned some things about him I didn't know and some things I did know, but what surprised me is that he understood who he was, probably better than any of us. Charles was an enigma because he was a person where the balance between good and evil was reasonably even, precariously perched, and ready to tip one way or the other based solely on his own indomitable will. It is impressive that a person with so much evil in them could will themselves to do good things. It wasn't a long stretch of time, but it was a solid four years from when he was captured in late-2253 until he jumped in late-2257, that he only did good things, and some of them were heroically good, especially his last, selfless act. The one that saved all of us.

A few days after his death, we gathered in Charles's backyard to say farewell to him. Before I go into the details, I'd like to challenge you with a question: How do you judge a person's life after they die? Is it simply an accounting of the things they did or didn't do? Their successes, their failures? Their good deeds and bad deeds? Or is it more appropriate to judge them based on how you feel about them? About him. That's the dilemma with Charles. He was a notorious criminal, one of the worst in the history of Earth. He literally destroyed the world. But then, he didn't because we changed history and pushed ourselves into another reality. The one we live in today. I can't tell you the number of times Charles thanked me for doing that, and I don't know if the law really means anything when it comes to Charles, but the law would have found him innocent due to insanity if he'd ever gone to trial.

And on top of that, how do you try a man for a crime he committed in a separate reality. It doesn't matter anyway. I ramble on about these things to give you some food for thought relative to what I'm about to tell you next because the memorial service for Charles ended up being a remembrance of all that he had done in his life, the good and the bad. Still, more than that, it came down to how we all felt in our gut about him.

Two thousand people were living on Base One at that time—1,500 Land People and 500 humans—and every single one of them was there. All fifty of the military residents were in full dress uniform, standing at attention directly in front of his house, and seven of them were equipped with rifles to send Charles off with a 21-gun salute at the proper moment. Speakers and video screens were erected on the streets so every attendee could see and hear what was being said. About two hundred of us fit into the backyard, where the service was held. A small stage had been built very close to the edge of the cliff, at the spot where Charles had jumped. We wanted to honor his bravery, so all of us who would speak would be standing very close to the edge too. A swift gust of wind might do to us what Charles did to himself. But Charles was a risk taker, and so were the rest of us who knew him well, except for, perhaps, Annette, bound by the rules and regulations of her post as the Minister of Time Management and Space Exploration, maybe the most powerful single person on Earth.

Annette came from Earth to join us. She'd known nothing of the going's on in 2749 until we'd told her because this Annette was from 2257. But it didn't matter what year Annette was from; she knew Charles, and she loved him, as we all learned, conclusively, from his book, and she doubled down on that love when she spoke at his service.

Charles's body was never recovered. We asked Cabal to mount a search for him, but he refused, saying that Charles was as much one of the Water People as he was of the Land People and humans, and it was the way of the Water People to allow their dead to become part of the food chain, under the water. From Cabal's point of view, there could be no greater honor for Charles than to be joined with the sea forever. So that is where Charles was laid to rest. In the seemingly endless ocean on the planet he had called home, Terrene.

All the time links were also there, except for Leah, who could never forgive Charles for holding her against her will for all those years. But the rest of them were there—Sophie, Aoife, Roisin, and Ciara. Even Eabha and Sadiki had made the trip. My parents had only met Charles once, during a visit to Terrene, so they stayed back on Earth, but they sent their condolences to those of us they did know.

There were four speakers at Charles's funeral, undoubtedly his four best friends in the galaxy. The first to speak was Liam Murphy. Liam approached the small stage timidly, taking slow short steps, his head bowed. I found it amusing, but not surprising that Liam carried with him not a paper with notes for his speech but a mug of ale. On the stage, he put both his arms behind his back and held the pint back there. He stood tall then, facing the crowd, and raised his head up high, but the creases of grief in his forehead and the redness of his eyes betrayed his deepest feelings.

"I s'pose I knew Charles as well as most, perhaps better than most," he said. "I first met him when I was a young man, in 1751, and it t'was Charles that introduced me to the love of my life." Liam looked down and smiled at Orla, who was in the front row, and she smiled back. "Indeed, I didn't have the chance to express my love to Orla until fifty years later, but it happened, eventually." The crowd chuckled. "Charles was part of that too. Without him, chances are Orla and I never would have met. After all, she lived on one side of the channel, and I lived on the other. But the reason we're all here is not about my story or Orla's; it's about all of our stories. Every one of us here crossed paths with Charles Burke at one time or another. So I ask you this: Is your life better because of meeting Charles, or is it worse?"

Liam gave the crowd some time to think about that, and as I looked out at the throng, I saw a lot of heads nodding and not one shaking from side to side. Liam could have ended his speech right there, but he had a few more words to drive home his message, almost as if he didn't want any of us to ever forget the impact Charles had had on each of us. "Charles done some bad things in his life," said Liam. "But from my view, I believe in my heart that more good came from his being alive than bad. It took some brave people, like Dani and Aideen and Annette, to make sure things went right, but in the end, Charles came round to the good side of life. And I say to you now, and I know you agree with me because I seen you noddin' your heads, that all of our lives are better because Charles was a part of them. A part of us, he was." Now Liam pulled his hands and arms from behind his back and held his pint in the air. Those in the crowd who had a drink with them, and there were many, raised it up. "To Charles!" said Liam.

"TO CHARLES!!!" returned the crowd.

Liam stepped slowly from the stage and gave way to Aideen. You all know that Aideen is a tough cookie, and there were no tears in her eyes as she spoke. She loved Charles as much as any of us, but she also had her pride, and her pride told her not to cry when giving a public speech. "Charles was the first and only boss I ever had," she said. "He built the Time Chain, using the first time travel technology ever invented, and did it on a shoestring budget." Chuckles from the crowd. "Of course, he deceived all of us time links from the start, and that still hurts a bit because I respected the man until I learned the truth of his intentions. But you know what, after it was all over and Charles was captured, he turned himself around. He did nothin' but good, for all of us, after that, and I say now, for all to hear, I have grown to respect Charles once again because he was a good man. Flawed, as we all are, but he willed himself to be a better person, and that's all any of us can do while we live in this universe."

Aideen stepped down, and I took the stage. My speech was short, but here is what I said:

"Charles was the smartest person I've ever known. And the bravest. I choose to remember the good, and while I won't forget the bad either, I choose to remember the good he did in this reality, and especially on this planet. I will miss him terribly."

Annette took the stage. She'd been a public speaker her entire life, but I'd never seen her so jittery. It was as if she knew what she had to say but didn't want to say it. But she gave it her best. "I'll just say up front that the good Charles was the love of my life. I read in his book that my future self, from 2749, told him that, so even though it took me five hundred years to say it to him, I'm glad I did say it before his life abruptly ended. We all know it was the good Charles that left us. Many of you here had the chance to see the bad Charles for a few ugly moments, here at the site of good Charles's last heroic act. Good Charles killed himself so that the rest of us wouldn't have to suffer at the hands of Bad Charles. As I said, it was a heroic act by one of the great heroes of Terrene and of Earth. Many of you know that Charles loved this place more than any other place he'd lived in, but he hated the name Base One. Therefore, a referendum has been drawn up by Clarion and Zephyr to rename this place, New Madagascar, in honor of Charles Burke, a servant of mankind."

Annette stood at attention, saluted, and the three rounds of the 21-gun salute fired, the bullets sailing over Charles's house and into the sea that had claimed his life and kept his body. The service ended, and everyone made our way to Murphy's pub to begin the grieving process by telling tales of Charles, the man who built the Time Chain, and much more.

*****

I was leaning up against the bar at Murphy's, one hand in the hand of the love of my life, Aideen, and the other holding a fresh pint of ale, when Annette approached us.

"You know, I read Charles's book," she said.

"And?" I responded.

"And I'm a little disappointed that I wasn't the real Watcher from the Sky!" Annette smiled, but I knew she wasn't finished. "Anyway, the question I have is, do you think that part of his book is, well, true?"

"That's a loaded question, Annette, and you know it," I said. "We all knew Charles could tell a story, probably better than any of us, including Liam. But sometimes those stories weren't completely true."

"But what about that particular story?" she asked. "The one about the Collection."

"I have no reason to believe it isn't true," I said. "But having said that, some things are just too big to get your arms around, Annette, and that sure sounds like one of those."

Annette went quiet for a moment, which all of you know is something she did when she was thinking really hard. And then she said something that I will never forget, something that got me thinking that maybe Aideen and I wouldn't be staying in retirement much longer.

"I think I know how to find them," she said.

Acknowledgments

Thank you to Sabrina Milazzo for her wonderful work on the cover design and the inside of the book.

About the Author

Steven Decker lives and writes in a small town in Connecticut, although he spends a lot of time in other parts of the world, and sometimes those places appear in his books. In addition to writing, he enjoys time with his family and his dogs and taking long walks in the countryside.

Made in the USA
Columbia, SC
05 April 2024

34032046R00137